"There's no need to insult me, Cambria.

"After all, we'll be seeing a lot of each other over the next two weeks."

"Oh, I see. You're the type that can dish it, but can't take it. Ain't that something!" She scoffed, then shook her head. "Let's make a deal. I'll show you the same level of respect you show me." She grabbed her handbag from the table. "So remember the next time you open your mouth, you can expect me to match whatever energy you throw out."

Miles watched her, silently surveying the way her glossy lips pursed into a straight line, the defiant tilt of her chin, the challenge in her eyes. She was mesmerizing, disconcerting even. No woman had ever affected him this way before. *She knocks me so off balance, but for some reason I like it.*

Her lips parted. "Why are you staring at me like that?"

* * *

What Happens After Hours by Kianna Alexander is part of the 404 Sound series.

Dear Reader,

Welcome to the fourth installment in my 404 Sound series. Now it's time for Miles, the "knee baby" of the family, to experience the magic of love. It's gonna be a bit of a ride!

Miles is focused on his family business and his charity work, which is near and dear to his heart. But how can he make his next event a smashing success? Enter Cambria Harding... Edgy, gorgeous and talented, she's nobody's angel. Working together for the good of the community is one thing, but can they find common ground outside the community center?

You'll have to read on to find out, and I hope you enjoy the journey.

Happy reading!

Kianna

KIANNA ALEXANDER

———

WHAT HAPPENS AFTER HOURS

HARLEQUIN®
DESIRE™

Recycling programs
for this product may
not exist in your area.

ISBN-13: 978-1-335-58148-8

What Happens After Hours

Copyright © 2022 by Eboni Manning

For questions and comments about the quality of this book,
please contact us at CustomerService@Harlequin.com.

Harlequin Enterprises ULC
22 Adelaide St. West, 41st Floor
Toronto, Ontario M5H 4E3, Canada
www.Harlequin.com

Printed in U.S.A.

Kianna Alexander wears many hats: doting mother, advice-dispensing sister and voracious reader. The author of more than twenty novels, she currently lives in her home state of North Carolina.

For more about Kianna and her books, visit her website at authorkiannaalexander.com or sign up for Kianna's mailing list at authorkiannaalexander.com/sign-up. You can also follow Kianna on social media: Facebook.com/kiannawrites, Twitter.com/kiannawrites, Instagram.com/kiannaalexanderwrites and Pinterest.com/kiannawrites.

Books by Kianna Alexander

Harlequin Desire

404 Sound

After Hours Redemption
After Hours Attraction
After Hours Temptation
What Happens After Hours

Visit her Author Profile page at Harlequin.com, or authorkiannaalexander.com, for more titles.

You can also find Kianna Alexander on Facebook, along with other Harlequin Desire authors, at Facebook.com/harlequindesireauthors!

For Tonya...the work continues.

One

As her jet-black SUV crept down Ralph McGill Boulevard Northeast, Cambria Harding gazed at the scenery rolling by from her comfortable perch on the back seat. The dark tint on the windows allowed her a look at her old stomping grounds while protecting her from the prying eyes of others. When she'd first begun traveling this way, in her black leather cocoon with a personal bodyguard and driver, she'd felt strange about it. But years in the music business had taught her much, and now she knew exactly why such measures were necessary to ensure she traveled safely.

The historic Old Fourth Ward neighborhood of Atlanta had morphed into something different than she remembered, yet was still recognizable. As they moved along the tree-lined streets, navigating through the thick traffic, she saw the new condominium developments dotting the landscape, towering over the older, more modest homes that had been around since her youth. There were businesses, both established and budding. Pedestrians strolled the sidewalks, some walking dogs of various breeds, and others simply striding toward some unknown destination.

She sighed. *It feels so good to be back here and not be working.* She'd done three separate shows in the metro Atlanta area over the past year, but she hadn't had time to chill on any of those occasions.

The last seven months had been filled with non-stop work: interviews, recording, photo shoots, and a multicity national tour that had taken her from Maine to Los Angeles and countless places in between. Exhaustion seemed too inadequate a word to describe how she felt.

A month of recuperation and spending some quality time with my granny is just what I need. "We're close, aren't we, Greg?" There was just enough new construction around her to make her question their exact location in relation to Granny Pearl's house.

Her driver and main bodyguard laughed, his deep chuckle filling the cabin. "Yeah. But you know how Atlanta traffic is." Gregory Alford, a native of Raleigh, North Carolina, had been a professional wrestler in the early aughts. Since retiring from his days as "Captain Crusher" a few years ago, he'd been putting his particular set of skills to good use by keeping overzealous fans out of her personal space.

The ringing of her phone grabbed her attention, and she slid it from the pocket of her jeans. Glancing at the screen, she swiped it to answer. "Blaine Woodson. Haven't heard from you in forever."

"That's because I know you stay busy, Cambria." His deep chuckle rumbled around her. "Where are you?"

"Actually, I'm in the A. Just pulled into town a couple of hours ago."

"Your timing is impeccable. My little brother Miles is doing a charity event, and he wants you to consider being a part of it."

Cambria tilted her head to the right. "Okay, but why didn't he call me?"

"He asked me to, since he doesn't know you that well." He paused. "Listen, my brother can be kind of…intense. But he's really passionate about his work to make life better for Black people in the city, especially the kids. I know it would mean a lot if you'd help him out."

She drew in a breath, considering his request. "Well, I'm technically on vacation. But I'm down. It is for the kids, after all. Just have him get in contact with me, and we'll go from there."

"Bet. Thanks, Cambria. Good looking out."

"Anything for an old friend," she teased, emphasizing the word *old*.

"Since you're doing me a favor, I'ma let that slide."

A few moments later she disconnected the call.

Another twenty minutes passed before the SUV finally came to a stop at the curb in front of the old but sturdy bungalow. As Greg helped her out of the truck, she inhaled the cool early September air, adjusted the dark shades over her eyes and stepped onto the wide wooden porch.

Before Greg could knock, the wooden door swung open, and a smiling face appeared behind the screen door. "Well, if it isn't my favorite niece." Lisa Harding, Cambria's youngest aunt and Granny's full-time caregiver, was only five years older than her. Lisa was dressed casually in black sweatpants and a white T-shirt, with a black-and-white-patterned scarf wrapped around the crown of her head. The blond ends of her shoulder-length bob hung from beneath the wrap.

Lisa opened the door wider and Greg swept Cambria inside the house. Once they were safely inside, Cambria drew a deep breath, inhaling the spicy scent of eucalyptus as she removed her sunglasses. "You're running the diffuser, huh?"

Lisa nodded. "When the weather turns cool, you know Mama wouldn't have it any other way." She chuckled. "That thing runs continuously from September to April." She reached out for Greg's arm and gave it a squeeze. "Always good to see you, Greg. Thanks for keeping our Sugar Plum safe."

He gave the same stoic salute he used to give when entering the ring as Captain Crusher. "She's easily the best boss ever, Ms. Lisa."

Greg took a seat on the worn beige sofa in the living room, as he always did when he brought Cambria to her grandmother's house, and the two women made their way to the back bedroom that Lisa had transformed into a combination sewing/TV room.

The low buzz of the sewing machine needle filled the space, but stopped as Pearl Radford Harding glanced in their direction. Seated in the old Queen Anne chair by the sewing table, she had been hard at work joining two quilt squares. A smile tilted her lips. "Sugar Plum. You made it."

Cambria moved to her grandmother's side and bent low, wrapping an arm around her shoulders. "Hey, Gran. How are you feeling?"

"Much better now that my baby is home." Pearl gave Cambria's waist a squeeze. "How was the trip?"

She stood again, grinning. "I took a private jet, so everything was great until Greg and I hit that famous Atlanta traffic. I swear, that's one thing about the city I just don't miss."

Lisa, leaning against the doorframe, added, "Every time I get stuck on that parking lot we call I-85, I fantasize about all the other places I could be living."

Taking a seat on Gran's beige easy chair, Cambria spent a moment enjoying the feel of being home. This room had once been her bedroom, but she certainly didn't begrudge her grandmother the space now. She owned three properties, one here in Atlanta, one in Denver, and one in a swanky suburb of Las Vegas, far removed from her parents' place in Reno.

The passing thought of her parents, with their Bible-thumping, sanctified attitudes and general disapproval of every life choice she'd ever made, was such a bitter one that she immediately pushed it away.

The sewing machine began to hum again and Lisa slipped out, leaving Cambria to enjoy Granny Pearl's company. "So, Gran, what's been happening around here since I've been on tour?"

"Let's see." She moved the fabric along the machine's plate with slow but deft hands, never taking her eyes off her work as she spoke. "Reverend Yarborough retired last month. We've got a new pastor now named Reverend Farmer. Nice young man, got a wife and a lil baby girl."

Cambria listened intently as her grandmother regaled her with all the gossip from church, her book club, and some of the locals Cambria had gone to high school with. When her grandmother mentioned her old singing partners, Eden and Ainsley, Cambria stopped her. "What's happening with them, Gran?"

"I said they both done married into the Woodson family. Eden married the producer you worked with, what's his name? Bart? Blake?"

"Blaine," Cambria interjected with a laugh.

"Yeah, him. Anyway, Ainsley married the other one, the one that runs the equipment and all that."

"Gage." She clearly remembered her interactions with all the Woodson siblings, even though so much time had passed.

"Yep, that sounds right. Anyway, they 'bout to have a gala at the end of the year, to celebrate thirty-five years in business. And that last brother, you know, the young one? He's been doing a whole lot of good work around here."

Cambria nodded, thinking back to the phone call she'd received. "So I've heard."

What kind of work is Miles doing? And how do I play into it?

Guess there's only one way to find out.

Seated behind his desk in his office at 404 Sound, Miles Woodson leaned forward, investigating the printed financial report he'd just received from the company's staff accountant. Scratching his chin, he reread the line of numbers he'd already read twice. Unfortunately, the numbers remained unchanged.

Profits on studio time are down 4 percent from August. He cringed, thinking of the recent expenditure for the new digital audio workstation now in use in Studio One, as well as the cost of the new soundproofing foam that had been added to both recording booths. Then there was the reflooring of the C-Suite to consider. And while he loved the new beige tile that had replaced the dingy nineties carpet in his office, he knew there would need to be some belt-tightening if profits didn't improve soon.

He shuffled around in his desk drawer for a bit, until he found the midyear report that had numbers from January to June on it. After studying it, he found a promising trend that gave him hope things would turn around.

Signing off on the August report and setting the papers aside, he got up and walked to his bookshelf. Locating the 404 Cares Community Foundation binder, he returned to his desk and began flipping the pages.

He frowned, noting the 22 percent drop in donations to the foundation over the last two quarters. Outside of his duties as chief financial officer for the family's recording studio business, he was also president of the company's charitable foundation. 404 Cares owned a small building two blocks away from the offices and studio, where Miles and a small staff made up of volunteers from within the company and students from local universities offered classes, entertainment and enrichment opportunities for local youth. One of his pet programs was Mindful Mediation and Self-Defense, which taught young people how to resolve their conflicts without violence, and to defend themselves if violence ever paid them a visit.

If I don't raise some money soon, I'll have to start cutting programming at the center. He wanted to avoid that if at all possible, and would even be willing to dip into his own pockets to do so. *Hopefully, this talent show will be a smashing success.*

He closed the binder, opened his laptop and clicked on the browser. Navigating to the home page of the local newspaper, he skimmed the weather report and the top stories displayed there. His eyes were drawn to a story about poverty among Atlanta's Black citizenry. Sipping from the blueberry protein shake in the tumbler on his desk, he read the article straight through, troubled by the statistics it mentioned. Joblessness, underemployment and hunger were running rampant in parts of the city where the population was mostly Black. And while so-called "urban renewal" had brought huge profits to some, many communities of color remained underserved and in some cases forgotten by the lawmakers charged with representing their interests.

He shook his head. *This is exactly why I do the work I do.*

On a new tab, he navigated to *Sweet Peach Tea Report*, one of the city's most popular yet shady gossip blogs. He scrolled down the home page, praying he wouldn't see his family or company mentioned. His prayer went unanswered, though, because he found an article about a third of the way down titled "404 Sound: Scandal Central."

Rolling his eyes, he clicked on the headline and opened the article. As he read the first few lines, he could feel his jaw tightening.

"404 Sound, the city's most legendary recording studio, owned by the wealthy and well-connected Woodson family, has seen more than its share of messy situations recently. Between rumors of an outside child fathered by the family patriarch, and this summer's in-studio brawl where two New York rappers threw hands like girls throw panties onstage at a Tank concert, it's beginning to look like the family business may not be as squeaky clean as we once thought."

Groaning aloud, Miles closed the tab. A brief internet search of the company name pulled up five other similar articles, one of which appeared in the *New York Post*.

Well, that's enough internet for today.

He closed the laptop and slid it away from him. He couldn't ever remember 404 receiving this much negative attention before, and he certainly couldn't imagine it happening at a worse time. They'd had their share of slipups and mistakes, like the recent lost equipment debacle that thankfully hadn't made its way to the blogs…yet. Damage control seemed too soft a term for what needed to happen to restore the family reputation before the thirty-fifth anniversary gala, and he worried he didn't have the fortitude to get it done.

A knock on his door drew his attention, and he swiveled his chair in that direction. "Come in."

The door swung open and Blaine marched inside. "Morning, lil bro."

"Hey, Blaine." He tried to loosen his expression, knowing he probably wore his stress on his face. "What's up?"

"I should be asking you that. Why is your face screwed up like that? You look like you've been sucking lemons."

Miles sighed. "I spent the morning looking over reports for both the studio and the charity. Let's just say I've got a lot of work ahead of me."

"You're not doing it alone, Miles. The whole family is here to pitch in, though sometimes I think you forget that." He flopped down onto the black leather cushion of the guest chair on the other side of the desk.

"I know that, logically. But between faltering profits, low donations and the gossip rags talking trash about us, it's looking pretty bleak from this side of the desk."

Blaine chuckled. "I'm guessing you saw that article in *SPTR*."

"You guessed right."

Waving his hand dismissively, he said, "Don't worry about them. They talk shit about everybody— that's kind of their business model." He paused. "I've got good news, by the way."

"Well, I could use some, so let me hear it."

"I talked to Cambria earlier today. Turns out she's already here in Atlanta on vacation, and she's agreed to see you to discuss being a part of the talent show."

For the first time today, Miles felt some of his tension melt away. "Really? Just like that?"

Blaine shrugged. "I told her it was for the kids, and that was all she needed to agree."

He sat back, sinking into his executive chair, and exhaled. "Great. When does she want to meet?"

He pulled out his phone. "She texted me her address and a time. I'll send the info to you now." He tapped his screen a few times.

Miles's phone vibrated on the desktop, and he picked it up and glanced at the screen. "Nine o'clock tomorrow."

"Right. And she warned me her security is on point, so you should expect a pat-down when you pull up."

He chuckled. "She is a major celebrity, so I guess that makes sense." Setting his phone down, Miles reopened his laptop. "Thanks for running point on this for me, Blaine. The kids in my defense class over-whelmingly voted for her as the celebrity judge for the talent show, so I know they'll be excited."

"So will any man or music lover in the Atlanta metro area, once word gets out that she's here." He laughed as he stood. "I gotta get back to work. I'm leaving early to take Eden to her prenatal checkup this afternoon."

Miles felt the grin stretch his lips. "I still can't imagine you as anybody's dad."

"Neither can I, but I guess I'd better get used to the idea," Blaine quipped as he headed for the door. "Later, bro."

"See ya." Navigating to the document he'd used to brainstorm the talent show, he made a few small tweaks, then printed it out, along with as much use-ful information about 404 Cares as he could find. Cambria had agreed to meet with him; the least he could do was be fully prepared to explain his mis-sion and purpose.

This event, and the funds it generated, would pro-vide warm coats, food and holiday gifts for fami-lies all over the Atlanta metro. And while Cambria Harding wouldn't have been his choice for celebrity judge of a kids' talent contest, she had a lot of local love and name recognition that would likely trans-late to ticket sales.

When it came to his community work, he would do whatever it took to make it a success. He had so many memories of happy Christmases growing up, and he believed all children deserved the same.

Two

Pulling the multicolored scarf tighter around her neck, Cambria held tight to her grandmother's arm as she entered the private waiting room at Sanderson Rheumatology. The staff had been kind enough to accommodate her unique situation by providing access to the rear entrance, and allowing them to go straight to the exam room to wait for Pearl's doctor to see her. Greg was parked in the lot behind the building, patiently waiting to drive them back home when they were done.

"Thank you again for bringing me to my appointment, Sugar Plum." Pearl eased into one of the two burgundy upholstered chairs.

Taking a seat next to her grandmother, Cambria smiled. "You're welcome, Gran. It's been so long since

I've seen you that I want us to spend as much time to-gether as possible while I'm in town." She also wanted to give her sainted aunt Lisa a break from being solely responsible for Granny Pearl's care, but saw no need to mention that aloud.

They sat together in the private room for a few minutes conversing, and Cambria watched her grandmother intently. She seemed a bit more frail and tired since the last time she'd seen her, and that was cause for concern. *I'm gonna be paying close attention to what Dr. Sanderson has to say today.*

The electronic hand sanitizer dispenser outside the door whirred, and Dr. Grace Sanderson entered the room, rubbing her hands together. Her slicked-back red hair and green eyes stood in stark contrast to her white medical coat and charcoal gray slacks. With her trusty laptop tucked beneath her left arm, Dr. Sanderson eased onto her stool and offered a welcoming smile. "Hello, Mrs. Harding. And hello to you, too, Cambria. Long time, no see."

"Hi, Dr. Sanderson." She chuckled. "What can I say? Life on the road is super busy."

"Yes, hello, Doctor," Pearl added in a small voice. "So what can you tell me about my latest scans?"

Dr. Sanderson nodded. "Sure thing. I took a look at your ultrasound, and I'm afraid there's quite a bit of disease progression of the arthritis in both of your hands."

Cambria felt herself wince, disappointed with the news. Her grandmother loved sewing, and if a time ever came where she could no longer work on her quilts, it was bound to have a detrimental effect on her quality of life.

Pearl frowned. "I was afraid you'd say that. I do the exercises you gave me, and I wear those hand braces most of the time when I'm sewing."

Dr. Sanderson's brow rose. "Most of the time?"

"At times I do forget." Pearl sighed. "Sorry, Doctor."

"Don't apologize. No one is perfect." Dr. Sanderson opened her laptop and navigated to the ultrasound images. "Here, you can see the damaged areas," she said, pointing with her fingertip. "How have your hands been feeling?"

"Stiff and achy, especially with the cooler weather."

The doctor offered a nod. "Yes, that's very common. Changes in barometric pressure and temperature often affect the joints, and it's especially noticeable when there is already disease present." She swiveled and began typing on the laptop. "I have a prescription in mind for you that I think will help with some of the stiffness."

Cambria's gaze swung expectantly to her grandmother's face. *She's not gonna go for that.*

Pearl balked, her lips thinning. "I don't like to take them pills, if I can help it. Too many side effects, and half the time you don't even know what's really in 'em."

"Understandable. Let's try this." Dr. Sanderson grabbed a small notepad from the desk and slid it close to her. Scribbling something on it, she said, "I'll recommend some natural supplements for now. Turmeric curcumin and glucosamine and chondroitin.

Give those a try, and see how you feel. If they work well, then we won't have to resort to any man-made pharmaceuticals. Deal?" She extended the paper toward her patient.

Her expression relaxing, Pearl nodded. "That sounds all right to me. But you'd best hand that paper to my grandbaby. I'm liable to lose it and forget what you said."

"Fair enough." Dr. Sanderson handed the note to Cambria, who tucked it into her Hermes Verrou clutch.

Soon they were back inside Cambria's SUV. After a quick stop at a local drugstore where they hit up the drive-through for Pearl's supplements, Greg drove them back to the little bungalow in Old Fourth Ward.

Standing on the front porch, Cambria leaned in and gave her grandmother a smooch. "I have a meeting now, but I'll be back later today, okay, Gran?"

"Okay. See you later, Sugar Plum."

She escorted Pearl to the door, where a smiling Lisa took her hand. "Come on in and let's get you some tea, Mama."

As she returned to the SUV, Cambria couldn't help wondering if Aunt Lisa ever felt resentful of her duties to Granny Pearl. Lisa was almost forty now, and as far as Cambria knew, she didn't have much of a social life. *At any rate, before I leave here, we're going to talk about this. I have money and resources to free up Aunt Lisa's time, and she deserves that.*

She rode in contemplative silence to her Buckhead condo. Located in a swanky, exclusive development called The Glades, her penthouse-level unit boasted private access via a separate entrance. A quick elevator ride from the parking deck deposited her at the door of her unit.

Once inside, she left Greg at his small desk in the living room and headed to her bedroom to freshen up. She expected Miles Woodson within the hour, and she wanted to look somewhat put together when he showed up. She ditched her dark sunglasses, setting them on her dresser. Eyeing her reflection in the wall-mounted mirror, she undid the scarf from around her head, fluffing her chin-length curls in an attempt to revive them. She'd gone to her grandmother's appointment dressed casually, and saw no need to change.

With a cup of coffee in hand, she sat down on the pink suede sofa in her living room and pulled out her phone. Realizing she knew very little about her guest, or his charity work, she put his name into a search engine to see what she could dig up.

Seconds later she found herself scrolling through a plethora of results. She paused at the first image of his face that popped up. *He's fine as hell…might be a little hard paying attention to his pitch if he looks this good in person.* Shaking her head at her own foolishness, she continued scrolling to inform herself of his good deeds.

By the time he knocked at her door, she'd read an impressive listing of community work. She nodded to Greg, who got up and opened the door.

Miles entered a moment later, dressed in a well-tailored navy blue suit and brown leather oxfords. His medium bronze skin, clear and glowing, spoke to a meticulous skin care routine, and his neatly trimmed hair and clean-shaven face indicated a decent amount of time spent in the barber's chair. But what really got Cambria were his eyes. Light brown bordering on hazel, they had flecks of gold and sparks of mischief in them that both intrigued and mesmerized her.

He approached her, at least as closely as Greg would allow, and his lips turned up into a sly smile. "Thanks for agreeing to meet with me, Ms. Harding."

A bit taken aback by his formal approach, she returned his smile. "You're welcome. You can call me Cambria, by the way."

He responded with a quick nod. "If you insist, Cambria. Shall we get started?"

Miles paused a few feet away from Cambria, allowing his gaze to sweep over her. She wore a pair of slim-fit black leather pants, a bright red top with sheer, gauzy sleeves that revealed a multitude of tattoos beneath, and black motorcycle boots. Her dark curls framed her face, grazing her shoulders and extending around her head in a similar fashion to the Afro his mother had worn in the seventies.

She began to speak then, and he watched her mouth, mesmerized. The words slipped like honey from between her glossy cherry lips, which flexed in time with her statement. Yet he heard nothing.

"Did you hear me, Miles?"

"I'm sorry, can you repeat that?"

She gave him just a touch of side-eye. "I said, I looked into your work and I'm impressed by what you've been doing for the community. I'm eager to hear about how I can help with your next project."

"Wonderful." He clapped his hands together. "Is there somewhere we can go to chat?"

She gestured to the empty space next to her on the cotton-candy-pink-hued sofa. "Just have a seat. We're not talking contracts or anything, so this will be fine." She paused, regarding him. "Are you cool with that?"

He heard himself stammer. "I just…d-didn't want to make things awkward…"

A deep voice filled the room. "No worries, playa. I'll be right here the whole time."

Swiveling his neck, he caught the eye of the big, bearded man who'd let him into the condo. *Must be her security. But why does he look so familiar to me?* Not wanting to stare at the giant too long, he snapped himself back to reality and took a few steps forward to join her on the couch.

She shifted her body slightly to the right, tucking her long legs beneath her. "So, Blaine tells me you have a really important event coming up, and you need my help."

He tried not to stare at the way the leather puckered over her thick thighs as he responded. "Yes, that's correct. I'm not sure if you know, but my family has a community center over in Westhaven. In addition to my CFO duties at 404, I run the center, overseeing several different programs. My main focus is youth enrichment."

She nodded, her eyes narrowing as an indication

of her interest. "Sounds like a worthy cause. It's always good when kids have a safe place to go. Keeps them outta trouble."

"That's the idea." He straightened his suit jacket, grateful he'd forgone a tie. Sitting across from a woman like Cambria Harding would have most certainly caused some kind of cartoon-level steam buildup under his collar. "My most popular program is all about mindfulness, conflict resolution and self-defense."

Bending her arms, she propped her elbows on her thighs, resting her noble chin on her delicate hands. "Tell me what that looks like."

He drew a deep breath, inhaling the soft floral scent of her expensive perfume as he did. "My main goal is to teach the kids to be present in the moment, to release worry about their reputations and the opinions of others, and to make sensible decisions even when they're frustrated or angry."

"Wow. Those sound like useful skills for the kids."

"They are." He paused. "I've seen way too many news stories about fights between kids in our community. Some are being bullied, some have an unstable home life… There's all these factors at play. Sometimes it's just a little scuffle but other times it escalates and someone ends up in the hospital…or worse." He shook his head. "I wanted to do something about it. I know my program isn't going to fix everything, but it's a start."

She nodded, a smile stretching her cherry lips. "I hear you. And I applaud your efforts. So many people see a problem and don't do anything about it beyond complaining, so you've got my respect. So tell me, how can I help you out?"

He mirrored her smile. "I'm holding a talent show as a fundraiser for this year's holiday project. We'll be providing groceries, warm coats and holiday gifts for thirty families in metro Atlanta."

"Awesome." She tilted her head. "Go on."

"I let the kids in my self-defense class vote on who they'd like as a celebrity judge, and you won by a landslide."

Her smile widened to a grin. "I'm so flattered. What's the average age of the kids in the class?"

"It's mainly middle and high school kids, so, twelve to seventeen." He paused. "Not sure they're your target demographic, at least not for some of your racier songs, but they really love your music."

Her expression changed for a moment, a frown flickering across her face. "Sounds like you're adding your opinion where it wasn't requested or required, my guy."

He cleared his throat. "My apologies. I didn't mean to…"

"Offend me?" She scoffed. "Don't worry, in order to be offended I'd have to actually care what you think." Her grin returned, as if it had never left. "At any rate, I appreciate their enthusiasm. I love all my fans, regardless of age or background."

He swallowed, feeling the tension gathering in his shoulders. *She's every bit as intense as her clothing and her music indicate, I see. If we're going to work together I need to be careful what I say to her.*

She straightened. "My next question is, when do I get to meet them?"

"Well, the talent show won't be held for a few weeks. I still need to do some organizing, get tickets printed up…"

She waved her hand. "No, I mean when do I get to come to the center and just hang out with them? They seem like cool kids… At least I know they have great taste in music." She winked.

He fought off the urge to roll his eyes, instead keeping his easy smile intact. Cambria's music was often sexually charged, full of foul language, or about other subject matter kids had no business thinking about. Yet she'd already made it clear she wasn't interested in his thoughts on that matter. "I'll set aside some time for that in the next class, if you're free. I'm sure the kids will be thrilled to meet you."

"When does the class meet?"

"Every Monday evening, six thirty to eight. Can you make it?"

"I'll be there. I'm on vacation, so my time is my own while I'm in town."

Thinking he could smooth out the bumpy edges of tension between them, he asked, "Is there anything I can do that will make your visit better?"

She shook her head. "I'm good. Just don't tell the kids I'm coming. I'd love to surprise them."

He nodded, thinking of ways he might let his students know they'd have a mystery guest coming to their class without giving away the secret. "I'll do my best."

Three

Bright and early Sunday morning, Cambria's car pulled up to the curb outside Granny Pearl's house. Greg was at the wheel, and Kenneth, an on-call security expert she often hired when she was in Atlanta, was in the passenger seat.

From the back seat, Cambria watched as Greg got out of the truck, knocked on the door, then escorted her grandmother to the vehicle. Once everyone was inside, Greg got them underway.

"Morning, Sugar Plum."

"Good morning, Gran."

Pearl eyed her granddaughter, letting her gaze sweep over her attire. Soon she smiled, giving a nod of approval. "You look right nice this morning."

"Thanks, Gran. So do you." She knew her grandmother felt right at home in her church finery. Pearl looked regal in her Kelly green skirt suit, dyed-to-match pumps, and coordinating wide-brimmed hat festooned with flowers and lace.

Meanwhile, these clothes feel like prison for me. Cambria had dressed as her grandmother expected and demanded, leaving aside her own preferences for the sake of peace and propriety. She wore a solid royal blue dress with long sleeves with a hemline well past her knees, nude pantyhose and low-heeled blue pumps. She'd tamed her mass of wild, dark curls into a low bun and secured it with a crystal hair clip.

"Did you bring your Bible?" Pearl asked.

She patted her blue handbag. "Right here."

"Good girl."

They rode in silence for the rest of the trip to Bethlehem Freewill Missionary Baptist Church, where Pearl had been a member for more than fifty years. As the four of them crossed the parking lot and ascended the front steps of the familiar brick structure, Cambria's mind traveled back to her adolescence, when her grandmother had her involved in just about every youth activity the church offered.

An older woman clad in the customary white usher's uniform welcomed them into the vestibule, exchanging smiles and greetings with them as she handed them each a printed program for the day's service.

As they entered the sanctuary, a buzz of conversation went through the small crowd of twenty or so worshippers, early birds who'd just finished Sunday

School and come up from the basement to snag the good seats before the church started to fill up. Most were women in their thirties and beyond, dressed similarly to Pearl.

They slipped into their seats in Pearl's usual pew, four rows from the front on the right side of the sanctuary. Pearl went first, then Cambria, who scooted her hips over the burgundy velvet as gracefully as possible to make room for Kenneth and Greg.

The pianist softly played hymns as a prelude to the service, while more and more parishioners entered, either coming through the door from the basement, or the main entrance in the rear of the sanctuary. As more people entered, more began to notice Cambria's presence.

She steeled herself for the onslaught. *Here we go.* Plastering on a pleasant smile, she greeted dozens of people who approached her, most of whom remembered her as little Cammy who used to sing for the choir.

"You used to sing so good the rafters shook," one man commented.

"Good to see you back in town. You know you're Pearl's pride and joy," one of the church mothers said.

She nodded and smiled and responded to everyone, and by the time the pianist played the opening hymn to signal the start of service, Cambria felt like she'd run a marathon. There was something about this particular setting, and all the memories tied to it, that seemed to sap her social battery much faster than most other public interactions did.

Reverend Farmer escorted his wife to the front pew, then took his place on the dais behind the altar while members of the choir filed into their seats in the stand.

Cambria tucked in her lower lip. *Granny Pearl's story checks out. He's pretty young, and his wife is very stylish.* Directing her eyes to the program, she busied herself reading it while bracing for the inevitable callout.

It came just after prayer, when Reverend Farmer asked all visitors to stand. After three brave souls in the now full sanctuary had introduced themselves, the pastor turned his attentions to her. "And let us not forget to welcome back a daughter of this congregation, who has gone on to much renown. Cambria, stand up, dear."

Doing as she was asked, she smiled and waved in response to the applause filling the space. When it died down, she retook her seat.

A trustee seated on the altar tapped the pastor's shoulder, whispering something in his ear. With a nod, the reverend said, "If I might be so bold...our elder says he would love to hear you sing, Cambria. And I'm inclined to agree with him. Would you come and sing a selection for us?"

Cambria stood again, taking in her grandmother's beaming face as she made her way to the choir stand to the sounds of more applause. Standing behind the microphone, she adjusted the height and angle of the stand before turning to the pianist. Speaking the song title softly, she then added, "F major, please."

Moments later, Cambria sang the familiar opening run to LaShun Pace's "There's A Leak In This Old Building." The song had been a favorite of her late grandfather's, as well as the one she was most often asked to sing lead on when performing with the Youth Mass Choir. The choir, though its membership had changed, joined in to provide flawless, practiced accompaniment. It occurred to her that these were likely the children of the young men and women she'd sung with more than a decade ago.

As she delivered the lyrics about the fragility of the human body and the glorious freedom of a soul taking its place in heaven, she let her emotions have their head. While she'd divested from organized religion in favor of a path that felt right for her, she'd never given up on her faith in a place beyond this life, an evolved state of being where all things would be made right and whole.

As she ended the song by holding out the last note, thunderous applause swirled around her, along with the sounds of banging tambourines and shouts of joy from the congregants. She stepped back from the mic and quietly returned to her seat while the spirit took hold of many in the pews.

Following her performance and the frenzied aftermath, the service segued into the offering and then the sermon. As Reverend Farmer preached about the Proverbs 31 woman, Cambria fought off her rising weariness. It wasn't just the singing and the socializing that had zapped her energy reserves, but the repetitive messaging. She'd heard this same sermon, remixed in one form or another, more than thirty times since her youth. *Men in the church never seem to tire of telling women how they ought to dress, behave and live their lives.*

As the sermon dragged on, Cambria excused herself to go to the restroom. Kenneth accompanied her up the aisle, walking a few steps behind her. Just as she passed one of the rear rows, she heard the whispering.

"Can you believe she'd even show up here? After all those years of making the devil's music?" asked one hushed female voice.

"Chile, she's all about loose living and whoring for attention," said another.

Cambria felt her jaw tighten. Kenneth's hand came to rest on the small of her back as she exited the sanctuary, indicating he'd also heard the two old hens' hateful clucking.

In the quiet of the vestibule, she fought back tears. Turning to Kenneth, she said, "I'm not going back in there. While I go to the restroom, let Greg know he can take Granny home after service. When I come out, you and I are leaving."

"You got it." He disappeared back inside.

Dejected, but not surprised, she slipped into the ladies' room, shutting and locking the door behind her.

Standing before the mirror in his sister's powder room, Miles stared at his reflection while washing his hands. His attention was drawn by the sudden, insistent buzzing of his phone in his pocket. *What could be so pressing on a Sunday afternoon?* Drying his hands, he slipped the phone out and looked at the screen.

Seventy-nine notifications? Swiping his finger, he checked the phone's queue, scrolling through them until he discovered the root of it all. Clicking on the video link, he leaned against the doorframe and watched Cambria belt out a popular gospel tune from the choir stand of a local church. According to the captions and hashtags, she'd performed the song during eleven o'clock service at Bethlehem Freewill Missionary Baptist. Even gospel sweetheart LaShun Pace had gotten wind of the video and left a positive comment.

He listened to the clear, strong quality of her voice as she sang, and was amazed by her talent. Sometimes, the production value of her songs on the radio seemed a bit over-the-top to him. Now it was obvious that was true. Studio backing tracks, with producers shouting over electronic drumbeats and looped samples, distracted from her talent. But with the stripped-down backing of a choir and a lone pianist, and those good old church acoustics, the true tone and quality of Cambria's angelic voice shone through at full splendor.

He'd watched the video three times when he heard Teagan call out. "Damn, Miles, what are you doing in there?"

Smiling, he closed the video, pocketed his phone again and went to the dining room.

He pulled up his chair to the table, grabbed the folded cloth napkin from his china plate and spread it over his lap. His stomach rumbled in response to the savory aroma of the food in front of him.

Nia, the eldest Woodson child and host of this little Sunday dinner, scoffed in his direction. "Still putting the napkin over your lap like a six-year-old, I see."

He stuck out his tongue. "Whatever."

Seated to his left, Miles's twin sister, Teagan, rolled her eyes. "Don't be such a stiff, Nia. It's just us today."

"Right," added middle brother, Gage. "Mom and Dad aren't even here, so there's no need to be so formal."

"She's not formal. Just uptight." Blaine, eldest brother, reached for a roll off the platter in the center of the table.

Nia slapped his hand with her spoon. "If you wanna talk junk, don't touch my yeast rolls, playa." Her voice was tinged with annoyance, but the crooked half smile and gleam of humor in her eye indicated that she was just joining in on the snarky sibling banter going around the table.

Miles chuckled as he looked around the table at the faces of his sisters and brothers. With their busy careers in the family business, and the recent marriages of Blaine, Gage and Teagan, it had become harder and harder to assemble them all in the same room at the same time. Apparently, though, they all agreed there was now a reason to upend their schedules and band together. The Woodson siblings were well overdue for an in-person meeting.

"Y'all go ahead and serve yourselves, then we'll get down to brass tacks," Nia announced, gesturing toward the food.

They passed around the platters of grilled salmon, garlic butter green beans, jasmine rice and yeast rolls. Once all their plates were filled, Blaine asked, "So, what are we gonna do about Mom and Dad?"

Nia sighed. "I don't know. But I feel like we have to do something. We can't just let them keep going on the way they have been ever since Keegan showed up."

Miles felt himself cringe at the mention of Keegan Woodbine's name. "We aren't a perfect family by any stretch. But I feel like we were doing just fine until he showed up with his wild paternity claims against Dad."

"What makes it so bad is…" Teagan paused, holding a forkful of rice in midair "…his claims may not be so wild at all."

Gage frowned. "Come on, Teagan. Don't tell me you believe that bozo. He's just a clout chaser and a scam artist, plain and simple."

Teagan went silent as she chewed and swallowed her rice. "I'm not so sure. As much as I love Dad, I know nobody's perfect."

Miles finished his salmon, then reached for his glass of iced water. He remembered the day Keegan had shown up at 404 with his accusations. And while he hadn't witnessed the event itself, he had witnessed the aftermath. Nothing could have prepared him for the hurt he'd seen in his mother's eyes. "I don't know if it matters whether or not Keegan is Dad's kid. Right now, we just need to get Mom and Dad talking again."

Blaine laughed bitterly. "How? Dad says Mom has been sleeping in one of the guest bedrooms for like two weeks now."

Nia sucked in her bottom lip. "That's not good. Usually when she gets mad with him she makes him sleep on the couch. If she was willing to give up sleeping on her expensive gel foam mattress, that means it's getting seriously bad between them."

Gage shrugged, his expression tight. "Who says we have to do anything at all? I'm not sure it's really our place to intervene or interfere with their relationship. After all, we're the kids. They're the parents."

Teagan stared at him. "That's incredibly callous, Gage. We're not kids anymore, we're all adults. And our parents are suffering. After all they did for us, the least we can do now is try to help them."

"Don't start, you two." Nia slid her empty plate away from herself, then folded her arms over her chest. "We'll settle this the old-fashioned way. Those in favor of staying out of it, raise your hand."

Gage's hand went up.

"Those in favor of helping out…" Nia began.

Four hands shot up.

Gage rolled his eyes. "I know, I know. Majority rules, so I'm in. I still think we're out of our depth here."

"That may be so. But doing nothing just isn't gonna work for me." Teagan sighed. "Where do we start?"

They spent a few minutes brainstorming, tossing around ideas that might encourage some positive interaction between their parents. Teagan acted as secretary of sorts, writing down the three best ideas on a sheet inside the small notepad she kept in her purse.

"It's not just the mess between Mom and Dad," Miles announced. "404 has had way more negative press lately than usual, and it's really hurting us."

"I know." Gage groaned. "I'm still so irritated that story about the stolen equipment got out. Not to mention what happened with my ex." He rested his forehead in his hand.

"You're telling me." Teagan shook her head. "I had grown men brawling in my studio like it was a professional wrestling ring instead of a place of business."

Miles nodded. "Exactly. This is just another link in a chain of unfortunate events that have brought us negative attention. Not only do we need to nip this thing with our parents in the bud, we also need to change the narrative surrounding our family business. This is our legacy."

"He's right," Nia added, standing up. "We can't let it all go down in flames, especially not so close to the thirty-fifth anniversary." She tapped her chin, her gaze drifting upward. "Let's throw as much support as we can behind Miles's work at the community center. We can't go back and change what's happened over the last several months, but we can do something good that will help us build positive social capital."

"Spoken like a true CEO, sis." Teagan leaned over to give her sister a high five, then turned to Miles. "So, how can we help you out at the center, twin?"

Miles felt the smile tilt his lips. "Oh, don't worry. I've got a million ways to keep you all busy. Trust me."

Four

Flanked by Kenneth and Greg, Cambria hurried across the parking lot of the 404 Cares Community Center in the southwest neighborhood of Center Hill.

Back in the day, Cambria had proudly repped SWATS as a member of the girl group SWATZ Girls, even though she technically lived on the east side with her grandmother in Old Fourth Ward. Eden and Ainsley, arguably her best friends in those days, were both from there, and that was enough for her.

It's been so long since I've been in SWATS. The scenery along Hollowell Parkway had changed, and a lot of that change hadn't necessarily been for the better. The sidewalks were cracked from lack of maintenance by the city. Overgrown vacant lots and dilapidated buildings were all too frequent. Yet in between those vestiges of blight, she saw hope. There were little storefront churches, busy restaurants, hair salons and other ventures making creative use of available space.

Now, as she walked briskly toward the community center, another such beacon of hope in the neighborhood, she couldn't help wondering why so-called "urban renewal" never seemed to benefit the people who needed it most.

The big two-story building housing the center had beautiful manicured landscaping and a newly paved parking lot. Its bright blue paint job with dark blue trim made it stand out against the austere gray of the autumn sky.

They entered the building through the door on the right side, as Miles had indicated. According to him, strolling through the front door would ruin the surprise before it got off the ground. Inside the building, Cambria hung back with Greg in the small multipurpose room, admiring the children's artwork displayed around her while Kenneth went to inform Miles of her arrival.

Kenneth returned a few moments later. "He says to just go through the door there." He pointed to a blue metal door to their right. "He's just told the kids they have a surprise guest speaker."

"And here I am without a speech prepared," she quipped.

Greg chuckled and held open the door for her.

She entered, with her bodyguards trailing her. Inside the large room, fluorescent lights reflected off the polished wooden floor dotted with those familiar blue vinyl mats. In the center, eight youngsters sat cross-legged on a group of pushed-together mats, with Miles seated in a folding chair in front of them.

"Our guest is here," Miles announced, gesturing in her general direction. "Let's give her a warm welcome."

Eight curious sets of eyes turned her way, and a moment later, the room echoed with the sounds of their screams and squeals of delight. Then they were all barreling in her direction.

Anticipating such a reaction, Greg stepped in front of her. "All right, lil homies," he called out. "Be cool. Go back and sit down, Cambria's coming to you."

As the children returned to their seats, Cambria sat in the folding chair vacated by Miles. Taking a deep breath, she smiled. "Hi. I'm so happy that I could come here and help you out with your talent show. But first, I wanted to meet you all and get to know a little bit about you."

One young girl, with tears in her eyes, said, "I'm Brandy and I love your music."

Cambria's hand went to her chest. Touched by her earnestness, she said, "Thank you. Nice to meet you."

"Jack and Kayla are gonna be so mad they missed this," a teen boy near the rear of the group said with a shake of his head.

Cambria giggled. "It's okay. I'll be back for the talent show, and probably before that. So anyway, let me hear it. Tell me your names and one cool thing about your life."

For the next few minutes, she listened as they introduced themselves. After finding out what they were willing to share about their hobbies and interests, she asked, "What do you like most about coming to the center?"

"I like this class. It helps me get my energy out," one of the younger ones said.

"Mr. Woodson looks out for us," one of them commented.

"Yeah. He always got the good snacks," added another preteen.

Cambria laughed. "That's definitely important. Can't thrive on lousy snacks." She glanced next to her and realized Miles was no longer there. "Where'd he go?"

Brandy pointed. "He's over there at his desk." Bringing her voice down to a whisper, she leaned in to add, "He's a cool dude but he's super serious, too."

Cambria turned her head and saw Miles seated at a small desk in the corner of the room. His lips were tight as their eyes met. *Why does he look like he's been over there sucking lemons? I swear, he has the same look Dad used to get before he launched into an epic lecture.* "Lemme see if I can get him to loosen up a little." Rising from the chair, she crossed the wooden floor, her steps echoing along the way.

"What is it?" he asked as she approached.

"That's what I came to ask you." She folded her arms over her chest. "I came here to meet your kids, to let them know I'm excited to be a part of what they're doing…"

"And I appreciate it. Really, I do."

She scoffed. "Well, I certainly can't tell. You've said ten words to me since I arrived, and you've been lurking over here in the corner for who knows how long. What's your issue?"

He leaned back in his chair, bending his arms and placing his hands behind his head. "Nothing."

She narrowed her eyes. "Nice try, but if that were true you'd be doing a lot less sulking and a lot more interacting." She stopped, recalling what he'd said when he visited her condo. "Is this about your funky little opinions about my music and my image? About how you think I'm not appropriate for kids?" She gestured to her black turtleneck and light-wash skinny jeans. "Most of my tats are covered, so what's the problem now? Should I have taken out my nose piercing, too?"

His deep sigh was followed by a change in posture as he straightened in his chair. "You're projecting. I'm sure your music and image are very carefully curated. So don't get mad with me because I pointed out the things you represent."

She took a step back, feeling her irritation rise. *He's way too good-looking to be this uptight, but I'm not gonna give him the satisfaction of saying that out loud.* "Look, I didn't come here for you. I came here as a favor to Blaine, and to support these kids. So I'm going back over there with them. Honestly, they're much more pleasant company than you are."

He stared, but didn't respond as she turned and walked away.

"What's up with him?" the kid who'd made the comment about snacks asked as Cambria returned to her seat in the folding chair.

She shrugged. "Who knows. He'll be fine, I'm sure. In the meantime, why don't y'all show me where he keeps all these good snacks y'all talking about." She looked to her guards. "Y'all hungry?"

"Always," Greg quipped.

Brandy stood up. "I'll run to the kitchen and be right back. Landon, come help me!"

As the two kids ran off, Cambria shook her head. *These kids are delightful. Their mentor, on the other hand, is too salty for his own damn good.*

And that's why I have to beat this pesky attraction to him.

Miles sat there for a few moments after Cambria walked away and began making a show of ignoring him. When he saw two of the kids running off, he stood and followed them to see what they were up to.

He found them in the kitchen, shaking down the cabinets. "What are you two doing?"

"Getting snacks," Landon answered as he pulled an entire basket full of individually bagged chips down from the top of the fridge. "We can, right?"

Miles sighed. "Sure. I did tell you guys to be as hospitable to our guest as possible. I suppose feeding her is part of that."

He watched them disappear with the chips and

a case of lemon lime soda, then passed through the kitchen into the main corridor. He walked toward the rear of the building and hung a right at the propped-open double doors of the Celestine T. Woodson Memorial Theater.

The room, which doubled as a space for performances and movie showings, was named in honor of his grandmother. As he walked down the center aisle between the two large columns of seats, he walked past the stage and entered the audiovisual room just beyond it.

Seated at the control panel, Teagan looked up when he entered. "Felt you coming, twin."

He rolled his eyes. "Whatever. How are you progressing?"

She watched him intently. "I'll answer that after you answer this. Why is your face so cracked?"

He frowned. "Not you, too."

She shrugged. "I'm just saying. You came in here looking like you got a whiff of something foul. Wait. Who else said something?"

"Cambria," he groused. "She's in the gym with the kids."

Her eyes widened. "Oh, she's here? I'm gonna see if I can get her to sign my CD cover of *Young, Wild and So Effin Free* for me." She grinned. "That album is still a vibe."

He sighed. "Okay. I answered you, so can you stop fangirling over Miss Freeway Threeway and tell me how the repairs are going?"

Teagan giggled. "All right. Chill out, saltbox." She

tilted her head to the right. "You know, when you said you had things for all of us to do around the center, I thought you meant passing out snacks or wrangling kids."

"Don't worry, you'll get to do some of that, too." He moved closer and patted his sister's shoulder. "Meanwhile you'll be saving me a mint by putting your tech skills to use to fix the control panel. Why pay a repairman when I've got an electrical engineer for a twin?"

"Lucky you," she quipped.

"I need that sound system in good working order before the talent show."

"I'm aware." She swiveled her chair back toward the electronic panel. "Seems to me like whoever installed this setup did a bit of a hack job. I'm probably going to have to get down underneath the panel and open it up to check the wiring."

"Yikes. How long is that gonna take? Because it sounds complicated."

"It *is* complicated." She slid the chair back and eased out of it, kneeling on the floor beneath the panel counter. "Fortunately for you, your twin is a genius." She grabbed the small silver key from its hook, to unlock the cabinet door. "It'll take me about an hour or so."

"Great." He started to turn and walk away, but her voice stayed him.

"Miles?"

"Yeah, sis?"

"Are you gonna tell Cambria you're crushing on her?"

He turned slowly in her direction, his gaze falling on her. "What?"

Shifting to a sitting position, she bent slightly to avoid bumping her head on the counter overhang. "You heard me. And don't say you don't like her. No sense in lying to your twin."

He groaned. "Don't feed me that line about us sharing an aura again."

"You said it, I didn't." She laughed. "So, are you going to tell her, or are you going to just keep skulking about like a spoiled kid?" She pulled out a screwdriver from the back pocket of her jeans and leaned into the open cabinet.

Miles drew a deep breath. "It doesn't matter if I think she's fascinating and infuriating at the same time. She'd never give a guy like me a second look."

"A guy like you? What do you mean? You've got a fan club from here to Columbus. You're out on dates with a different woman every other weekend. Now suddenly you meet someone who's a little famous and you lose all confidence?"

"It's not that. I don't care that she's famous." He ran a hand over his close-trimmed curls. "We work in a studio. We meet famous people all the time."

"True, true." Her voice echoed as it bounced off the walls inside the cabinet. "Oh, I think I see the problem. You're used to women being so impressed with your looks and your status that they just fall into your arms. Ms. Harding ain't doing that and now you're pressed."

I hate when she does that. Her tendency to read him like a newspaper column had always unsettled him, and what made it worse was that she was pretty much always right.

"Your silence tells me I'm right." Her entire torso had now disappeared inside the cabinet.

He sighed aloud.

"Anyway, you don't have to tell her you like her if you really don't want to. But you are gonna have to improve your attitude around her. She's helping you out, after all. The least you can do is not be a jerk." Something metal clattered to the floor. "Dang it. Miles, grab that metal tube that just rolled away from me."

Spotting the silver cylinder on the floor, he walked over and retrieved it. Sticking it into the cabinet for his sister to grab, he said, "I'll do my best. It's not just that I think her music isn't appropriate for the kids…"

"I'd advise you not to actually say that to her, but knowing you, you already did."

He decided to ignore that not-so-subtle dig. "Anyway, it's a combination of things that has me really tense. I'm just worried something will go wrong and derail my plans for the talent show before I even get them off the runway."

"I get it. Adulting is hard, and you're a little on edge. Book a damn massage and stop taking it out on someone who's doing you a favor. Sheesh."

"I guess I should do that." He scratched his chin.

"When I look at her, all I can see are headlines about our volatile relationship and subsequent breakup hitting the blogs and social sites."

She slid back until her head was out from under the cabinet and stared up at him. "Miles, you're so uptight you're already catastrophizing a relationship that doesn't exist. I'm gonna need you to find your chill, and find it quick. Your anxious foolishness is starting to harsh my mellow, bro."

He chuckled at his sister's weird turn of phrase. *Sounds like something Dad would have said to one of his buddies back in the day.* "Well, I'll leave you to your tinkering, then. Just come find me when you're done."

"Roger that," she said as she disappeared back into the cabinet.

He walked away but paused at the door. "Thanks for the advice, sis."

She laughed. "Thank me by taking it."

Shaking his head, he left the AV room and headed through the theater and back out into the hallway.

Five

Cambria lay in bed Monday night, propped up against the wealth of pillows behind her. Dressed in one of her favorite nightgowns, she had a charcoal mask on her face, a terry wrap around her hair and her e-reader in hand. As she read through a cozy mystery novel, sipping ginger and turmeric tea between pages, she enjoyed the feeling of relaxation washing over her.

This is the first time I've really felt like I'm on vacation since I got here. It was half past ten and she'd been comfortably ensconced in the covers for the past two hours. *I'll get up in the morning and go see Granny. But for now, I'm on DND, IRL.*

She looked up at the sound of a gentle tap against

her doorframe. "I'm headed to bed, Cambria," Greg said. "Need anything before I turn in?"

"No, I'm good. Good night, Greg."

"Night, Cambria." He disappeared as quietly as he'd approached.

Engrossed in the story now, she let her mind run through all the suspects that had been presented thus far. Unable to come up with a solid guess at the culprit, she merely shook her head and kept reading.

Her phone rang then, and she frowned, realizing she'd forgotten to silence the ringer. Reaching to the nightstand to grab it, she answered it when she saw the name on the screen. "What's up, Harley?"

"I see you're enjoying your vacation, Cambria." Harley Harrison, her longtime business manager, released a chuckle. "Seems the parishioners at Bethlehem Baptist were very excited to have their favorite soloist back." Harley kept up with her schedule and bookings, and also managed her money, since she was a certified public accountant.

Cambria scoffed. "I don't know about that. I'm just a local girl made good, indulging my granny's wishes to come to service with her." Not everyone in the crowd had been pleased to see her, and even though she wanted to forget, the cruel words of those two old biddies were still stuck in her brain.

"That was quite a different look for you," she added.

"I know." Cambria cringed at the memory of her church clothes, but took some solace in the fact that as soon as she'd gotten home, she'd snatched off those itchy, confining pantyhose and tossed them right in the trash. "Granny's very conservative, so I just dressed in a way she'd approve of." And hated every second of it.

"At any rate, your appearance in the choir stand was very well received and the video has gone viral. It's had over three million views on MyVid."

"Yikes, I didn't realize it had gotten that popular." She hadn't looked at the stats recently. "Last I saw it was still in the thousands."

"You're trending on social media, and your song streams and downloads have ticked up a percent or two, all off the strength of that solo." Harley clapped her hands together several times. "Brava, diva."

"You know that wasn't intentional. But I guess I'll take the benefits from it."

"You should. And you should also think of other ways to build goodwill with the fans."

She sighed. "I'm on vacation, remember, Harley? I know it's rare for me to take time off, but I'm officially off the clock right now."

"You're never really off the clock, though, sugar." Harley's tone changed to something less chipper and more serious. "You've reached a certain level of fame now. There are certain sacrifices that have to be made if you want to maintain it."

She sucked her bottom lip into her mouth. "I've sacrificed plenty. Have you forgotten my forty consecutive weeks on tour, while doing interviews, promo, photo shoots? That's exactly why I need this vacation."

"I don't mean to ruffle your feathers. But your success is my success. That's why I'm so passionate about it."

Commission is a hell of a motivator, I see. Shaking her head, she said, "I'm doing some work with a local charity while I'm here."

"Oh, that's perfect. What will you be doing?"

She gave her manager a brief rundown of her role as guest judge for the talent show and the purpose for which funds were being raised. "An old friend asked me to do it as a favor, and it made sense to say yes. Participating won't eat up my whole vacation, and it's a good way to give back."

"I agree. Forget everything I said earlier about you doing more. Turns out you're doing plenty." She paused. "What's important now is that you build some great connections, both with the young folks, and with whoever's running this whole enterprise. We could always use the good press."

She let her head fall back against the pillows as she thought about the man behind the event. Miles seemed to irk her nerves at every available opportunity, but she couldn't seem to rid herself of her attraction to him. "I'll do my best. I met with the kids earlier today, and I think they're pretty awesome."

"That's just the kind of thing you can say to interviewers when this is all over. You know, how much you enjoy charity work, and how much you love the kids. All that good stuff."

She cringed as Harley drifted off into "manager speak." It was as if a whole new node of her brain lit up, turning off all other thoughts outside of those that led to some tangible benefit. "Remember that show where you had the vendors trade merch for donations to the food bank? That got you so many brownie points in the industry."

"Yeah, I remember. It was great to be able to help out so many families." That one-night-only show in Raleigh had raked in a few thousand dollars for the local food bank. She hadn't been thinking of how she'd benefit when she planned that show. Her mind had been on helping people, on using her platform for good.

"I know someone else is in charge this time, but I want you to put the same amount of positive energy into this as you put into your charity show."

"Don't worry, Harley. I've got it covered."

"Well, keep me posted on how this event turns out. I won't bug you again since you're on vacay, but feel free to reach out when you're up to it."

"Awesome. Thanks, Harley." After they said their goodbyes, Cambria ended the call and replaced her phone in its spot on the nightstand. Closing her e-reader's cover, she set it aside as well and used her fingertips to massage her temple.

This was some hell of a day. From this morning's failed attempt at incognito grocery shopping, to her meeting with the kids, clashing with Miles and now that slightly irritating call with her manager, it had been eventful on many levels.

The exhaustion of the day was quickly catching

up with her, and she knew she'd be snoring within the next twenty minutes.

She made a quick trip to the bathroom to peel off her mask and brush her teeth before slipping between the covers again.

Flicking off her bedside lamp, she punched the pillows a bit to plump them, then resettled herself into their down-alternative fluffiness.

"Mr. Woodson, did you hear me?"

Looking up from his phone screen, Miles met his secretary's confused gaze. "No, I'm sorry, Tisha. Can you repeat that?"

"I said, Blaine called and said he'll be up in the next few minutes."

"Thank you, Tisha."

She left the room, and in the aftermath, Miles looked back at his phone screen.

Closing the site, he locked his phone and set it aside. Soon after that, Blaine strolled into the room. "What's going on, Miles? You still haven't assigned me any duties at the community center. You do know I'll be glad to help out if you tell me what you need."

"I know. I just haven't figured out how to make the best use of your talents yet." He gestured to the seat across from him. "Is that why you wanted to see me? To ask to be put to work at the center?"

"That's one of the reasons. Have you seen the social sites this morning?"

He shook his head. "No, I haven't. I've been avoiding most of them for several weeks now. After so many stories painting us in a bad light, I just had to let that go."

"I know all that. I also know you peek at them occasionally when curiosity gets the better of you."

"How do you know that?"

"Teagan. How else?"

"I can see it's time to have another talk with her about using her twin sense to put me on blast." He swiped his open palm over his face, from forehead to chin. Slightly recovered, he asked, "What did you see on social media that you wanted to tell me about?"

"We're getting so much positive attention now that people know Cambria's in town, and that she's agreed to work with the students." Blaine took out his phone, then began scrolling. "One of the kids snuck a video of Cambria eating chips and drinking soda at the center last night, and it's getting a lot of views."

"Isn't it funny how people can get excited about anything done by a celebrity, no matter how innocuous?" He chuckled.

Blaine eyed him. "Whatever, man. Her little innocuous actions have caused 404 Cares to be a trending topic on three different social sites."

His eyes widened. "Are you serious?"

"Just open up the apps and see for yourself, Miles."

Doing as his brother asked, he could see that the company community foundation was indeed trending. "Wow. I gotta check the donations portal." Once he logged in, he filtered the results to see the donations that had come in over the last twenty-four hours. "Damn. Our donations are up twenty percent, just since yesterday."

"Shouldn't that boost take care of the families we agreed to help?"

He shrugged. "Probably. But if we keep working, it also means we can help more families. I didn't tell you this before, because it's somewhat depressing. But beyond the thirty families already chosen, I have eleven more on a waiting list." He scratched his chin. "I'd love to come up with enough money to clear the waiting list, as well."

"That's awfully noble of you, bro."

"I don't see it that way. You, me and the rest of our siblings grew up blessed. I think it's only right to pass some of that on to the community, to let them know that someone cares about them."

"You're a good man, Charlie Brown," Blaine teased. "But seriously, though. Whatever you're doing, keep it up."

Miles scratched his chin. "Honestly, it isn't anything I've done to get that level of increase in donations. It was you, for reaching out. And Cambria, for agreeing to help."

"You're giving me too much credit, bro." Blaine drummed his fingertips on the desk. "I haven't always done what was best for the family, and we both know that. This was such a small, easy thing, so I'm glad I could come through for you. Still, she wouldn't be here if you hadn't met up with her and explained your mission."

He sighed. "I guess I did close the deal. I just wish I felt better about who the kids chose."

Blaine pursed his lips and stared. "Nah, Miles. You not about to do that."

"What?"

"That judgy thing you do. Where you decide what someone is worth based on your perceptions."

"But I don't…"

Blaine held up his hand and shook his head. "Lemme stop you right there. We're not even going down that path. The bottom line is, let go of your need to judge. See Cambria as a person, and stop sizing her up by her public persona. Okay?"

"I feel like I have no choice but to agree," Miles replied, rolling his eyes.

"In life, you always have a choice. You can either agree to do what I'm telling you, or I can give you an early lunch…a knuckle sammich." He slowly raised his fist like a supervillain before a confrontation. "What's it gonna be, bro?"

Miles snorted a laugh, and soon his older brother was laughing along with him. "All right, I yield. I don't want smoke with you."

"Good choice." Blaine unclenched his fingers and dropped his hand back to the desk's polished surface. "Now, I'm gonna ask again. What do you need me to do around the center?"

Miles leaned back in his chair, tapping his chin as he thought about it for a moment. "You know what? All things considered, I think you'd make a pretty good youth advisor."

Blaine tilted his head, his eyes widening. "Really? Don't you usually have therapists and social workers do that?"

"I do. But there's always room for someone with life experience and wisdom to impart." Miles nodded, feeling good about his decision. "I think this will work especially well for some of my teen boys. They don't necessarily want to talk to Dr. So-and-So, because that seems too formal or intimidating to them. I think you may be able to relate to them in a way that will encourage them to open up."

"Wow. I'm low-key flattered you think of me that way." His big brother grinned.

"Hey, look what you've been doing for me all these years? Hell, for all of us, except maybe Nia—she's too headstrong to take advice."

Blaine snickered in response to that quip. "You right about that."

"Anyway, yes. I feel very confident in your ability to listen to these young men, to make them feel seen and heard, and give them sound advice when they ask for it." He paused. "You've got the skill set—I've seen it firsthand. Even though you can be annoying as hell, we couldn't ask for a better big brother."

Blaine's grin widened. "Thanks, Miles."

"You're welcome, though I'm just speaking facts."

The two brothers shared a double fist bump before Blaine left the office, leaving Miles alone with his thoughts.

He's never steered me wrong before. I'm gonna try to take his advice.

Six

"Awesome. Greg's back with the food."

Cambria looked up from her phone at the sound of her aunt Lisa's voice, just in time to see her bodyguard walking toward her dining table with two large white plastic bags from Hattie Marie's Texas Style BBQ. She clapped her hands together. "Yassss." Her stomach growled in anticipation as the spicy, savory aroma of the food touched her nostrils.

"Considering how crowded it was in there, I'm impressed by how quick they brought this out." Greg set the bags down on the table between the two women.

"Did you get yourself something?"

He nodded, taking a tray out of one of the bags. "I love their brisket, so I got that."

"Cool. Grab yourself a drink if you like." She gestured to the bucket of ice on one end of the table, in which she'd placed several cans of soda and bottles of water.

"Thanks. I'm gonna eat at my desk so you two can have girl talk." Grabbing a bottle of water, Greg disappeared around the corner, headed back for the living room.

"You don't mind him eating in there with all that light-colored carpet?" Lisa asked, sipping from her glass of iced tea.

She shook her head. "Nah. He's grown, and he rarely ever makes messes. You sound like Granny, asking me that question."

Lisa laughed. "I'm with her most of the time, so I guess she's rubbing off on me."

Cambria pulled the bags close to her and began unpacking them. With each container she opened and sat in the center of the table, she became surer that she'd chosen the right outfit for today's lunch: a long-sleeved red tee and a pair of super comfy black sweatpants. When everything was unpacked, she sighed. "I probably ordered too much food."

Lisa chuckled, unrolling her silverware. "Probably. But it all looks so good I can't blame you."

"My eyes were definitely bigger than my stomach today," she admitted. She'd ordered crab clusters, fried lobster tails, a full slab of ribs, macaroni and cheese, collard greens and corn bread. "Oh, well. At least I'll have leftovers to nibble on for the next few days."

Already piling food onto her clear crystal plate, Lisa nodded. "Nothing wrong with that. Plus, you supported a local business and that's always a good thing."

Taking a swig of ginger ale, Cambria fixed her own plate. A few moments later, she groaned as her taste buds reveled in the mingling flavors. "This is so freaking good. I never get to eat like this on tour."

"That's probably for the better. Otherwise you'd be too full and sleepy to perform." Lisa forked up some of the well-seasoned greens.

"True."

"I wanted to ask you something, about that event you're doing."

"The talent show?" She eyed her aunt over the sauce-drenched rib in her hand. "I don't know all the details, but I'll try to answer you. What do you want to know?"

Leaning forward with a mischievous grin, she said, "I'm not asking about the event so much as I'm asking about the organizer. Are you really working with Miles Woodson, the local golden boy?"

Cambria snorted a laugh. "Yeah, although I wasn't aware he had that much sway around here."

"I mean, all the Woodsons have a certain level of status around these parts. The studio has been around forever, and there's definitely name recognition." She bit into a lobster tail and chewed. "That's pretty good. Never had one fried before." After a couple more bites, Lisa continued, "Anyway, I just saw Miles's name in a regional magazine. It was one of those roundup stories, you know. 'Top Twenty Most Eligible Bachelors in the Southeast.'"

She felt her brow hitch. *Oh, no. Auntie about to activate Matchmaker Mode. Her eyes are glowing and everything.* "All right, I'll bite, because I know you're gonna tell me either way. What number was he on this list?"

"Number four." She dunked the last bite of lobster in the little plastic cup of butter. "They referred to him as handsome, wealthy and community-minded. A girl could do a whole lot worse, you know."

Chewing a mouthful of mac and cheese, she took some time to think about how she would respond to her aunt's well-intentioned yet obvious meddling. By the time she'd swallowed the cheesy goodness, she had the perfect response. "Aunt Lisa, you're not that much older than him, and you're single. If you really think he's a good catch…"

Lisa held up her hand. "No, ma'am. Don't turn this one back on me. I like my men a little older, a little more blue-collar, a little rougher around the edges."

She shrugged. "Okay, fair enough."

Lisa chuckled. "You're really something, Cambria. I just want you to have someone to come home to when you come off the road, you know?"

"I do." She smiled. "You and Gran."

"You know what I mean."

"I know. You mean something more romantic." She polished off the last of her corn bread. "I've spent enough time with Miles to know we're not suited for that kind of thing."

"Why not?" Her aunt's frown indicated genuine disappointment.

"Honestly, he's uptight, judgmental and a little bit full of himself." She rolled her eyes as she thought back on their interaction the previous evening. "He's just not my type."

"I see. But if you think he's attractive…" Lisa let her voice trail off, and her gaze shifted ever so slightly to the side.

Cambria feigned shock. "Auntie! I know you're not suggesting that type of behavior. What would Granny say?"

"First of all, Mama's not here." She laughed. "Second of all, I know my favorite niece ain't about to dime me out to her. All I'm saying is, he's fine, y'all both young and whatnot. You been working so hard. Ain't nothing wrong with a lil distraction, chile."

"I could say the same thing about you, Auntie." Cambria pushed away her empty plate and sipped the last little bit of her soda. The ice rattled as she sat her glass back down. "You've been taking care of Granny full-time for two and a half years now. When are you gonna take some time for yourself?"

Lisa leaned back in her chair, lacing her fingers together and placing her hands in her lap. "I do take time for myself. Besides, I love taking care of Mama."

"I know you do, and Granny is lucky to have you. But don't you think you deserve more time to yourself?"

"I'm the only daughter she has," she insisted. "It's what's expected of me. It's what's right."

Cambria shook her head. "It's expected, yes. But do you really think it's fair that you're the only one looking after her out of her four kids? Just because the others are sons?"

Her aunt's gaze lowered, and she remained silent.

"It's like I said—you've been amazing to Granny. But I make enough money now to pay someone to look after her…"

"No," Lisa snapped, pounding her fist on the table. "She's my mother. I won't pawn her off on a stranger."

Fully aware of all the ways Black women often laid their bodies down at the altar of self-sacrifice, Cambria reached across the table. "You didn't let me finish, Auntie. They could come in part-time, just to give some relief."

Joining hands with her niece, Lisa spoke again, her voice soft with emotion. "I…suppose that would be all right. I just love Mama so much. She deserves the best, and sometimes I'm afraid she won't get that from anybody else but me."

"I get that. Granny's amazing and she does deserve the best. Between the two of us, we'll see that she gets it." Squeezing her aunt's hands, she added, "Since you were willing to consider my offer, maybe I'll take your advice about 'distraction' under advisement, too." She winked as she released her grip.

Lisa laughed heartily. "That's my girl."

* * *

Tuesday evening, Miles sat across from his father in a booth at Vining's Southern Steakhouse. The upscale, intimate restaurant had a prime midtown location, and decor featuring an eclectic mix of African and South American art that created an elevated atmosphere.

He glanced up from his perusal of the menu laid on the table in front of him, but couldn't see his father's face due to Caleb's penchant for holding his menu in front of him. "Any idea what you're getting, Dad?"

Clearing his throat, he said, "Not yet, son."

"Take your time." Miles returned his attention to the selections, lingering on a few particularly tasty options.

When the waiter returned to replenish their water glasses, they placed their orders, with Miles requesting the surf and turf with a baked potato, and Caleb, steak frites with a Caesar salad.

"Your mother is always on me about eating my veggies," Caleb said after the waiter left. "So I added a salad. Maybe that will get me some brownie points."

"It's a start." Miles took a long draw from his water glass.

"Thanks for meeting me, son." Caleb leaned back on his seat. "Your mother hasn't been cooking for me, and I was tired of eating sandwiches and pizza."

He smiled. "You're welcome, Dad. It's no problem, really." While he had mixed feelings about everything happening between his parents, as it stood at the moment, he had no real reason to avoid his father's company.

"So, tell me about your talent show project. How's that coming along?" Caleb grabbed a roll from the basket on the table, and took a bite.

"It's going pretty well. I've got the kids working on backdrops for the stage, and perfecting their acts. Teagan came over and fixed the control panel for the lighting and sound in the theater room, so we're good to go there."

"Benefits of having an engineer in the family," Caleb said with a chuckle.

"Absolutely. She saved me a mint on a repair tech. But I think the biggest thing happening on the talent show front is that Cambria Harding is on board, and she's drawing a lot of attention to our event."

"Yes, I heard. I'm glad to see she's willing to help out. It's bound to make your fundraising efforts a lot more fruitful."

"It already has. We've had a noticeable increase in donations since word got out that she's involved." He thought back to Monday night, when she'd visited the center. "She came to the class this week, and the kids were over the moon with excitement."

"Excellent." His father's smile indicated his genuine pleasure with the news.

Their food arrived, and they each spent a few minutes enjoying their dinner. Miles savored the well-seasoned, perfectly cooked steak, and enjoyed the flavor and texture contrasts of the grilled lobster tail, and the warm, fluffy interior of the baked potato.

"So what's she like?" Caleb cut through a piece of his steak. "Is she easy to work with?"

"Yes and no," Miles admitted. "Some of that's on me. At times, I don't know how to reconcile my opinion about her music with how much the kids love her." He shook his head. "It's just too mature for kids, you know?"

He shrugged. "They're kids. Appropriateness will never have any bearing on their tastes. They just like what they like. It's been that way for every generation. This one is no different."

He could see the truth of his father's words; after all, he'd listened to his share of foul language and sexually explicit music when he was in his teens. "You make a good point. Anyway, to answer your question, she's pretty easygoing, but definitely not afraid to speak her mind. She can even be a little snippy at times."

"That's a good quality in a woman." Caleb chuckled around a forkful of salad. "There are no shrinking violets in the Woodson family, that's for sure."

He laughed, too. "Yep. Mom, Teagan and Nia are all about that life." He paused. "Cambria's gorgeous, too. Even better-looking in person than she is in pictures."

"Sounds like you're attracted to her," Caleb announced.

He hesitated, then admitted, "Yes, I am. Can't seem to shake that feeling of utter fascination with her, no matter what I do."

"Remember, son, Cambria is a celebrity. Men all

over the world are enamored with her. You should keep that in mind before you get too carried away." He pushed his empty plate aside. "Don't get so caught up that you lose sight of your goal."

"Noted." Miles sat with his father's words for a few moments. *Guess I'll have to move carefully when it comes to Cambria.* He'd had a lot of plans in mind when he asked Blaine to reach out to her; becoming a member of her fanboy contingent was not among them.

"You know, I heard from Travis this morning."

Miles's ear perked up at the mention of the family lawyer's name. "Really? What did he say?"

"He said that lab has finished the in-depth DNA test he ordered, and the results will be delivered to Nia's office by courier over the next few days."

"That's good." He stopped, confused. "Wait. Why is it being sent there, instead of to you?"

He sighed. "Your mother doesn't trust me not to try to hide or tamper with the results." The corners of his mouth drooped, and his eyes held sadness. "Three decades of marriage, of building sacred trust—all shattered by some scammer off the street."

Miles took a deep breath. "Well, once the results come in, at least the issue should be resolved, right?"

"You'd think that. But with everything that's happened, it may not be so easy to return to the way things were." Caleb drummed his fingers on the table. "Your mother no longer trusts me, and there will be fallout from that. I expect we'll need counseling, at the very least."

He nodded. "Makes sense. I'll try to support the two of you in any way I can."

"I'm glad to have your support, son." His father sighed. "It means a lot to me, even more at a time like this." He chuckled, his gaze resting on a faraway point. "You know, the day I married your mother, I made a solemn vow to be faithful to her. And ever since that day, I've kept that vow."

He kept quiet, sensing that his father had more to say.

"Your mother is the best thing that ever happened to me. She deserves my loyalty, and so much more." Caleb paused. "I don't know if you or anyone else believes me when I say I never strayed. But I know in my heart that I've been true to my Addy. And that clarity of conscience…it's more important than anything."

He watched his father's face, saw the sincerity in his eyes. It made him wonder why Keegan would make up such a lie, especially one that could be so easily disproven.

Seven

Cambria sat down on the plush cushion of the wicker sofa and sighed as she sank into its softness. It was a beautiful autumn Wednesday, and the breeze flowing around her rooftop terrace could only be described as heavenly. In the relative quiet of the early morning, where only the song of birds and the buzz of traffic ruffled the silence, she inhaled deeply and let herself be filled with inner peace.

After spending a few minutes in quiet meditation, she returned inside her condo to get dressed for the day. Donning a pair of navy leggings, a yellow, long-sleeved crop top and a brown vegan leather vest, she added a pair of brown knee boots. After fastening a thin gold chain around her neck and matching hoops in her ears, she swept her curls into a high ponytail.

Strolling into the living room, she grabbed her handbag from the hook by the door, and let Greg escort her to her car.

On the drive toward Collier Heights, she watched the scenery and thought about what this day might hold. She'd gotten a rather unexpected call from Miles, inviting her to meet him at the coffee shop near the 404 building to discuss plans for moving forward with their talent show collaboration. When she'd reminded him of how difficult it was for her to have meetings, or even linger for more than a few minutes in a public place, he'd responded that he'd booked the coffee shop for a private event. No one would be allowed in or out for two hours other than those he designated, he'd explained.

Now that she was on her way to the coffee shop, she had to admit she was impressed with the extra effort he'd taken to assure her privacy and comfort. *Maybe he does this all the time, since he's got a lotta pull around here. Either way, I feel kind of special that he set it up for me, without my team needing to do anything.*

They arrived at the Bodacious Bean a few minutes before eight. True to Miles's word, there were only two cars in the parking lot; she assumed one to be his and the other to belong to store staff. Looking inside through the windows along the front, she saw that all the tables were empty, except for the one occupied by Miles.

Greg stepped back as she approached the counter and ordered a slice of banana bread with a medium

KIANNA ALEXANDER 75

roast coffee. He then trailed her at a respectable distance as she eased over to the table where Miles sat. She let her gaze sweep over his well-dressed frame, clad in a pair of coal black slacks, matching vest, a long-sleeved purple button-down and a purple-and-black paisley tie. He draped one foot over one strong thigh, showing off his polished black wingtips. Easing into the chair across from him, she said, "Good morning."

"Good morning to you," he replied, offering her an easy smile. "You know, it took me a while to figure out why your bodyguard looked so familiar. Man, it's so cool you have Captain Crusher as your protector."

She giggled. "I agree. Thanks for doing this, by the way." She gestured to the empty tables around her. "I appreciate it."

"You're welcome. I thought you might like a change of scenery. Plus, when we're finished, it'll only take me five or ten minutes to get back to the office." He winked.

"Are you gonna have anything?" She posed the question as Greg delivered her items to the table.

"I already did. Had a coffee and a croissant before you came." He gestured to the half-full bottle of spring water on the table. "This is all I need for now."

"Cool. So tell me, now that I'm on board, what are your plans for advertising the talent show to the masses?"

"Mostly through social media. I feel like that's the easiest and most cost-effective way to reach people nowadays, at least in the demographics we're targeting." He rested his elbows on the table. "Will you be willing to post about it on your accounts?"

"Sure, that's not a problem. I do think you should add radio to your promotional strategy, though. And maybe the local news stations."

He scratched his chin. "I'd considered the local news, but not the radio. It probably won't even cost that much to run a few commercials on the local hip-hop and R&B stations to drum up interest."

"When is the talent show, anyway?"

"Two weeks from Friday." He sucked in a breath through his teeth. "It's a pretty short lead time. I'll probably have to pay for rush production on any radio commercials I run, but it could very well be worth it."

"I think so. And you don't need to do anything special for the news, just convince them you've got a story, and let them interview you."

He tilted his head, watching her, his eyes slightly narrowed. "I'm impressed. You talk like a true marketing maven."

She shrugged. "After all these years in the music business, I've picked up on a few things, believe me." She picked up her ceramic mug, blowing some of the steam away. Taking a tentative sip, she sighed. "This coffee is amazing. And I can tell they made it just like I asked. Sugar-free caramel and oat milk."

"We Woodsons don't pay for coffee anywhere else. The Redfields, who own this place, have been friends of my family for years now. Nobody brews quite like them."

She took another long sip before sitting the still-hot cup down. "So, we'll let people know via the news, radio and social media. Other than judging the night of the show, is there anything else I need to do?"

"You can act as a mentor to contestants who'll be singing."

She nodded. "I don't have a lot of experience with that kind of thing, but I'll give it a shot."

"I think your wealth of industry experience will be more than sufficient." He touched his fingertips to his thumbs, circling them against each other. "I do have one concern. Have you cleaned out your social accounts lately?"

She felt her brow furrow. Unsure of what he meant, she asked, "Can you clarify that, please?"

He cleared his throat. "What I mean is, you've had a lot of past involvements, and a couple of messy public breakups. It would probably be better if obvious evidence of those things is removed."

Heat rose in her throat, making her face hot as irritation got the better of her. "Stalker much?"

"I don't mean any harm by it. It's just… I've been in business long enough to know that you should check out people you plan to work with."

"Humph." What a convenient excuse to go nosing around someone's personal matters. "And I doubt many people pass your little inspection."

He blew out a breath. "So have you updated your social media, or not?"

"No, I haven't, and I don't plan to. I am who I am. My real fans know about how pain can breed beautiful art."

"It breeds beautiful souls, as well," he added in a low voice.

She wanted to speak, but stuffed a piece of banana bread in her mouth, forcing herself to chew as she carefully chose her words. "That's cute. But if you really believe that, then why have you been finding me lacking in some way ever since we met?"

Miles felt his shoulders tense beneath her intense gaze. "I apologize to you for that. It was rude of me to express my thoughts that way."

Her eyes flashed. "Expressing your thoughts? It's bad enough you made these snap judgments in the first place. If you think the problem is that you were impolite, then you're not as astute as I assumed."

He rubbed his temples. "There's no need to insult me, Cambria. After all, we'll be seeing a lot of each other over the next two weeks."

"Oh, I see. You're the type that can dish it, but can't take it. Ain't that something?" She scoffed, then shook her head. After a few moments of silence, she spoke again. "Let's make a deal. I'll show you the same level of respect you show me." She grabbed her handbag from the table and pulled it into her lap. "So remember the next time you open your mouth, you can expect me to match whatever energy you throw out."

He watched her, silently surveying the way her glossy lips pursed into a straight line, the defiant tilt of her chin, the challenge in her eyes. She was mesmerizing, disconcerting even. No woman had ever affected him this way before, confounding and fascinating him all at once. *She knocks me so off balance, but for some reason I like it.*

Her lips parted. "Why are you staring at me like that?"

Shaking himself free of her spell, he slid his chair back from the table. "Sorry. I was…considering your offer."

"So, do you agree? Because we need to settle this now, or we're not going to be a very effective team for your talent show."

"Then I agree. This event will be the key factor in my ability to help as many families as possible, so I'll do whatever is necessary to make it a success."

Her expression softened considerably, until a ghost of a smile tipped her lips. "I see the passion you have for the community. It's a passion I share… and I really respect it."

Finally, a crack in the ice. "Thank you." He gave her his most charming smile, the one that usually made women melt like candy on a hot day.

She laughed. "You're welcome. You can stop cheesing at me now, though." Setting her mug on the crumb-sprinkled saucer, she asked, "Is there anything else we need to discuss?"

He blinked a few times as realization hit him. She hadn't been affected at all by his toothy smile, other than finding it goofy. *Damn. I don't really know what to do with that.* "Uh, no. That was basically it. I just wanted us to get a strategy together on promotion."

"Well, I think we've got that covered." She eased back from the table and stood. On cue, her guard stood from his own seat a few tables away.

"Thanks again for coming." He walked around to her side, closing the physical space between them. As he came near her, the soft, amber scent of her expensive perfume washed over him, dulling his sense just a bit.

But not enough to keep him from noticing the change in her guard's stance. In his peripheral vision, he clearly saw the retired wrestler's body language change from casual to protective.

She raised her hand behind her head, holding up her index and middle fingers.

The big man dropped the bravado right away.

She dropped her hand, letting it come to rest on his shoulder. "You're welcome, Miles. Greg is very cautious when it comes to me, and history has shown that's for the best." She lowered her eyes beneath a thick fringe of dark lashes, then raised her gaze to meet his again. "I'd advise you to ask me before you breach my bubble next time."

"I will…and I'm thrilled you're alluding to a next time."

Her brow hitched. "My, my, Mr. Woodson. You've certainly changed your tune."

"You were right. We need to be able to get along if we're gonna work together for the success of this event." He made no attempt to hide his regard as he raked his gaze over her shapely frame, which, despite her relatively casual dress, still drew his interest on every level. "And the more time I spend with you, the more I realize I want to get along with you."

She laughed again, shaking her head. "You're something else, Miles. Are you seriously flirting with me right now?"

"The fact that you're asking that makes me think I'm not coming on strong enough." He stared at her face, at the glowing, unblemished skin above the line where her neck tattoos began. "Is it all right if I touch you? I don't want your bodyguard to do a finishing move on me."

She nodded. "Keep it appropriate and it's fine. Get too handsy, and I give him the signal to expose your organs to daylight." Her tone held humor and teasing, but he had no desire to test the seriousness of her honey-glazed threat.

Raising his hand, he dragged the tip of his index finger down her cheek. Her skin, even softer than he anticipated, felt like crushed velvet beneath his touch. Not wanting to drag it out too long lest he awaken her ire and the wrath of her dragon protector, he let his hand fall away.

Her tongue darted out and swept over her lower lip.

"Am I good?" he asked softly.

"Yeah, you're good." Her response, low and breathy, tempted him to repeat the gesture. She wrapped her hand around his wrist and stayed his hand, moving it to the curve of her neck just above her shoulder. "This is a dangerous game you're playing with me, Miles."

"I'm not playing at all." His gaze landed on her lips and lingered there. Seeing the slight tremble at the corners of her mouth thrilled him. *The smile wasn't enough, but I'm on the right track now.* "I'm very much serious...as serious as you'll allow it to be."

She sucked in her lower lip briefly, then released it. "You know, my aunt said something to me yesterday, and I think I'm starting to see the wisdom of her words."

Curious, he swirled the pad of his thumb around at her collarbone and asked, "What did she say?"

Her gaze fixed on his, intense and purposeful. "That there's nothing wrong with a little distraction."

"I think I like where this is going."

She eased a little closer. "You and I aren't compatible for a relationship. But I think we could definitely infuse a little fun into this charitable partnership—" she eased closer still "—as long as we both understand that a distraction is all we can ever be to each other." She slid her open palms up his arms, the warmth of her touch permeating the silk-blend fabric of his sleeves, until they came to rest on his shoulders. "Do you think you can do that? Be my distraction?"

Sliding his arms around her waist, he heard himself growl, "Absolutely."

A moment later, she raised her chin and their lips crashed together. Soon their tongues were twisting and mating, and he could feel his breaths become ragged and uneven as his body reacted to the woman in his arms.

She eased away from him, brushing her pinkie over her full lips. "I'll see you later, Miles." She turned and started walking toward the door, with her bodyguard trailing.

He nodded. "Okay. I don't want to monopolize your day."

Stopping by the door, she turned her head and tossed back, "You will, though. And you'll do so with my permission." Giving him a sultry look, she said, "Be at my place in an hour."

A moment later, the bell chimed as she and her guard slipped out.

Standing in the empty coffee shop, with the scent of her perfume still clinging to his clothes, all he could do was grin.

Eight

Back inside the confines of her condo, Cambria slipped out of her boots and tucked them into her coat closet.

Lingering in the doorway, Greg said, "I'm gonna guess you want me to make myself scarce, right?"

She chuckled. "Yeah. Take some personal time. I'll give you a call when I'm ready for you to come back."

"Cool. I'll hang around until he gets here to give him access to the elevator. Even after that, I won't be far away if you need me." He slipped out, shutting the door behind him.

Locking up, she went to her bedroom to change. Peeling off her clothes, she stripped down to nothing. Doing a little turn in the mirror, she admired the shape of her body, as well as the quality of her tattoos.

Turning slightly to the side, she paused to admire her favorite one, the image of Shenron the Eternal Dragon that took up the entire right half of her back. She'd loved anime during her childhood, finding the fantastical story lines made a great escape from the oppressive reality of living with her conservative parents. Going over to a friend's house to watch *Dragon Ball Z* had been one of her favorite modes of subtle rebellion, at least in those days.

She entered her closet and chose a comfortable gold-and-black silk caftan that covered her from shoulders to ankles, and slipped into it. Wrapping her hair in the matching scarf, she slid her feet into a pair of black fuzzy house slippers and headed down the hall toward her theater room.

Once inside, she flipped on the lights. The room, quiet inside except for the hum of the mini-fridge in the concession area, was outfitted with four charcoal gray love seats. All the seating faced a projector screen flanked by red velvet curtains, which occupied an entire wall. She could control the Wi-Fi-connected digital projector built into the opposite wall, with an app on her phone.

She slipped behind the concession counter and opened the fridge to check what beverages were inside. She hadn't used the room in months, due to her relentless touring schedule. *Even the last time I was in here, I was watching choreography footage, trying to learn steps for a show. It's been way too long since I used this room for recreation.*

Satisfied that there were enough drinks inside,

she closed the fridge and spun around to start up her old-fashioned popcorn machine before settling onto one of the love seats in front.

The sounds and aroma of the popper filled the room as she made herself comfortable. She searched through her digital film collection on her phone until it chimed to alert her to Miles's presence at the door. Switching apps, she viewed his handsome face on the screen for a moment, then swiped to let him in.

She heard the door open and close, and called out to him. "I'm back here! Follow my voice."

He entered the theater room and whistled. "Wow. This is a really nice setup."

"Thanks," she said, turning toward him. "It's impractical for me to go to a theater nowadays, so I brought the theater home."

"Makes sense." His brow hitched as he moved closer to her. "You changed."

"Just getting comfortable. I hope you don't mind my lil mumu." She let her gaze sweep over him. He'd gotten rid of his vest and loosened the top few buttons on his shirt; those were the only changes to his outfit.

He ran his hand over his chin. "No, I don't mind it at all."

He'd mind it even less if he knew there's nothing underneath. Smiling at that spicy thought, she said, "Help yourself to popcorn. You can grab a drink from the little fridge back there, too." Gesturing to her armrest cupholder, she added, "I've got my ginger ale already." He turned and strolled to the concession counter.

She watched with appreciation the way the fabric of his slacks stretched around his strong hips and thighs as he moved. "There's a few of those big cardboard popcorn buckets in the cabinet under the popper."

"Gotcha." He grabbed a bucket and filled it with freshly popped corn. "Butter?"

"There's a dispenser built into the counter. It automatically heats up when the popper is turned on. Just look for the little nozzle…"

"Oh, I see it." Shortly, he joined her on the love seat and handed over the bucket of popcorn. Slipping a bottle of orange soda into the cupholder near him, he asked, "So, what are we watching?"

"If Beale Street Could Talk." The film, adapted from the James Baldwin novel of the same name, had become one of her favorite romantic dramas. "Have you seen it?"

"I have. My mom is a huge Baldwin fan, so we all watched it in the family room at my parents' house when it came out on digital."

Queuing up the movie, she changed position and sat crisscross, dropping the popcorn bucket between her thighs. "Then you know how good it is."

He nodded, settling in next to her and grabbing a handful of popcorn.

As the movie played, Cambria felt herself drawn into the world of the story for the umpteenth time. The onscreen chemistry between Kiki Layne and

Stephan James could only be described as electric, and Regina King's Oscar-winning role in the film proved every bit as moving as at her first viewing.

Even as riveting as the movie was, she couldn't ignore the less-than-subtle undercurrent of desire flowing between her and Miles. He'd draped his arm around her shoulders, and she realized she was lying on his chest but had no idea how long she'd been in that position.

Tilting her head, she looked up at him and found him watching. Wordlessly, he cupped her chin with his large hand, his firm yet gentle touch capturing her face.

She swallowed, unable to tear her eyes away from him.

"Can I kiss you?" His words, low and gruff, stroked something inside her that had been asleep for a long time.

She nodded. "Please do."

He leaned down and pressed his lips to hers. This wasn't like their earlier kiss in the coffee shop. No, this kiss was deeper, more intense. Earlier it had been all fun and games, but in this moment, he kissed her as if he had something to prove.

He drew her into his lap, the bucket of popcorn falling to the floor. She gave no thought to the spilled contents as she let herself be enveloped in his arms and in the masterful movements of his tongue inside her mouth. Her hand went to the back of his head and he groaned against her lips.

Beneath her hips, she could feel the hardness

that indicated his growing desire. Her own body, encased inside her silken garment, became slick with her blooming need.

He pulled away, his breaths heavy. "You know, if we keep this up, we're not gonna finish the movie."

She shrugged. "We've both seen it, no big deal."

He stroked her cheek, his big hand covering the entire side of her face. "Didn't you say you're here on vacation because you had a brutal touring schedule?"

"Yes, I did." She pecked him on the forehead. "It's nice to know you were listening."

"I'm very observant of things that matter to me." He licked his lips. "I also noticed you've been yawning throughout the movie."

She blinked a few times. "I didn't even realize that."

He gave her waist a squeeze. "Listen. I'd be lying if I said I didn't want to bend you over the armrest right now." He trailed his finger down her throat, over her tattoo of the Shikon Jewel and down between her breasts. "But you are tired, Cambria. Maybe too tired to be sure you really want this…"

She shook her head. "Nah. I'm sure I want you."

"Fair enough, but I can tell you're still too exhausted for me to make love to you the way I want to." He paused. "The way you deserve."

"What do you mean?"

"I mean that when I take you down, I'm going to take my time. I'm going to kiss every place that needs my attention. I'm going to make sure you cum, as many times as your body can handle." He gave her hip a squeeze. "Trust me, you will need your full strength."

She stared, so turned on by the implications of his words that she couldn't speak.

He gave her another peck on the lips, then slipped from beneath her. "Give me a call when you're fully rested, and I'll take care of you, all right?"

She nodded, her eyes locked on the bulge in his slacks.

Minutes later, he departed, leaving her alone with her thoughts. She couldn't help admiring his self-control, while realizing how much he'd tested the limits of hers.

This certainly went beyond my anticipated level of distraction... I won't be able to concentrate on much else until I test this man's skills.

Seated on the sofa in the family room of his child-hood home Thursday evening, Miles did his best to temper the tension he felt rising inside him. He'd left his office and gone home only long enough to change into dark green sweats and white sneakers before coming here. They were all about to get an answer to their most pressing question, but at this point, he wasn't sure he even wanted to know.

Gage sat to his right, and Teagan to his left. Across from them, Blaine lounged on the matching love seat, scrolling through his phone. Their father, Caleb, re-clined in his favorite armchair nearby. Their mother, Addison, was seated at the piano near the entrance to the dining room. Miles watched for a moment as she absently picked out the tune of Bizet's "Habanera" from *Carmen*. It had always been one of Addison's favorite compositions, but Miles could tell his mother's playing lacked any passion or nuance.

No one said a word, and he assumed by their expressions and their mannerisms that they were all feeling similarly anxious. Letting his head drop back against the sofa cushion, he stared into the tray ceiling above him. His mind replayed snippets of the many happy memories he'd made with his family in this room. There were movie nights, game nights and many a spirited debate about one topic or another. Birthdays with balloons and singing. Easters and Thanksgivings enjoying his mother's delicious homemade dishes. Christmases unwrapping gifts and drinking hot cider while a fire roared in the fireplace.

So many years, so many moments of joy. There had been sorrow, too… He clearly recalled Addison comforting them all after their grandmother, Caleb's mother, had passed away. They were about as close-knit as a family could be, and the foundation of that lay in the love that their parents shared.

Is all that about to change? Are we about to lose the glue that holds this family together? Considering the way their mother had been acting toward their father of late, Miles thought his fears of a family implosion were well-founded.

Teagan's voice broke the tenuous silence. "For heaven's sake, where is Nia?"

"Chill, sis. She probably got caught in traffic or something." Blaine barely looked up from his phone.

Miles shifted his gaze to his father's face again, and he noticed how weary he looked.

The sound of the front door opening and closing echoed through the house, and everyone looked toward the foyer.

Nia entered the room then, shrugging out of her jacket as she walked. "Hey, y'all. Sorry it took so long. Traffic was outrageous."

"Called it," Blaine announced.

"Well, do you have?" Teagan scooted up to the edge of the sofa cushion.

Nia nodded. "Yeah, I have it." Reaching into her purse, she pulled out an envelope. "I haven't looked at it. I just stuck it right in there when the courier delivered it."

"Let's get this over with, Nia." Addison ceased her playing and swiveled on the piano bench, her eyes locked on her eldest child. "Open it up and read it."

"Please do," Caleb added. "I'm ready for this whole mess to be over."

Nia blew out a breath. "Okay. These results are from Legacy Diagnostic Labs, who came very highly recommended by our family lawyer." She fumbled a bit as she unfolded the envelope to full size, then used her acrylic nail to tear it open. Removing the paper inside, she held it in front of herself at chest level. Clearing her throat, she read aloud. "In reference to the paternity of Keegan Wilson Woodbine..." she paused, her lips moving almost imperceptibly as she skimmed "...the alleged father, Caleb Ivan Woodson, is *not* excluded...as the biological father of the tested subject." She stopped, swallowed, her expression grim.

"Oh, fuck." Gage began massaging his temple.

Nia began speaking again, her voice trembling. "Based upon analysis the probability of paternity is 99.99…"

Miles felt his heart pounding in his chest. He felt many things, but the overwhelming sensation was one of anger. He clenched his fist, using his free arm to comfort Teagan, who quietly sobbed next to him.

"How could you, Daddy?" Teagan asked before turning her face into Miles's shoulder.

His twin sister's pain felt as palpable to him as his own, and as he gave her a gentle squeeze, he felt his anger strengthen. How could Dad do something so selfish?

Caleb leaned forward in his chair. "That can't be right. It can't be!" He reached for the paper, which his daughter handed over without protest. "What is this? It's lies! It's all lies from the pits of hell!"

Addison screeched, her hand flying to her mouth. Everyone looked her way.

Slowly, she rose from the bench, tears streaming down her face. Slipping off her wedding rings, she set them on top of the piano and started to walk out toward the foyer.

"Addy, please." Caleb grabbed her arm as she passed him. "It's not true, I swear. There has to be some mistake…"

"Save it, Caleb." Their mother's voice quaked as she spoke. "If after all this time, you still can't bring yourself to tell the truth, to take responsibility for what you did…" She turned away without finishing.

Nia grabbed her mother's hand. "Wherever you're going, that's where I'm going."

"Me, too." Teagan stood, slipping from Miles's embrace. Then the three Woodson women left, not even looking back at the sound of Caleb's protests.

Alone with his sons, Caleb continued to speak. Beads of perspiration formed on his forehead as he spoke. "Call our lawyer. Tell him we need to redo the test. Tell him it's not right…"

Gage shook his head, a look of disgust on his face. "It's over, Pop. Give it up."

"No! I'm not giving it up because I didn't do this!" His voice climbed an octave as he stabbed the air with his index finger. "I didn't cheat on my Addy. That boy isn't my son. And I…I…" Caleb's eyes began to dart around the room, his breathing uneven and labored. When he spoke again, barely above a whisper, he said, "I…can't see."

Then his eyes widened and rolled up in his head. His upper body careened forward.

"Dad!" Blaine shouted, rushing to grab Caleb before he tumbled out of the chair. "Somebody call an ambulance!"

Miles whipped out his phone and dialed, never taking his eyes off his father's slumped form.

Nine

Cambria grabbed Greg's offered hand and stepped down from the back seat of her SUV. It was Thursday evening, about an hour after darkness had shrouded the city, and half that amount of time since she'd gotten the brief yet alarming text from Miles.

Can't come over. Dad in hospital.

She'd immediately jumped into action, searching until she found a news report about Caleb Woodson. Then she'd dressed quickly in a black hoodie and sweats, dark sunglasses and black sneakers. Now, as she quickly crossed the parking lot of the hospital with Greg in tow, she wondered what she would encounter when she actually got inside.

Everything she knew about the Woodsons indicated that they were a close-knit family, and she imagined the sudden illness of their patriarch would cause major strife among them. And Miles, as businesslike and stiff as he could be, was likely beside himself with worry.

I know we're not in a relationship. But I feel like he needs someone right now and I'm in a position to be there for him.

In the reception area of the emergency department, she waited while Greg tried to get information on Mr. Woodson, and discreetly revealed her identity. One nurse immediately left the bustling desk and escorted them down a corridor to a staff elevator. "I'll have to go with you since only staff are supposed to use it, but I'll take you straight there."

"Thank you," Cambria offered as they slipped inside the elevator car.

The moment the doors closed, the nurse began to squeal. "I can't believe *the* Cambria Harding just randomly showed up at my job. Like, what are the odds of that? They gotta be astronomical. Can I please, please have your autograph?"

Despite her anxiety over the situation, Cambria felt that warm feeling of fan-love wash over her. "Sure thing, hon." Smiling, she grabbed the marker she saw sticking out of the nurse's scrub pocket, as Greg handed her one of the laminated tour passes he carried around for her. Reading her badge, she wrote her a personalized autograph. "Here you go,

Markisha. Hold on to that, because anytime I'm in Atlanta, it'll grant you access to the VIP section."

The young woman's eyes widened, and she squealed again. "OMIGOSH! Thank you so much!" She tucked the pass carefully into her lower right pocket, moving her knees back and forth in a sort of excited happy dance.

The elevator dinged as it reached the fifth floor, and the doors slid open.

"Mr. Woodson is in room 517," Markisha informed them. "Just got admitted maybe twenty minutes ago. It's down the hall, to your right." She'd shifted back to professional mode, but the tinge of excitement remained in her voice.

"Thanks again," Cambria said as she and Greg stepped off the car. "See you at my next ATL date, all right?"

Markisha grinned, and as the doors closed, Cambria heard her squeal once more, the sound echoing in the elevator shaft.

Greg chuckled. "Gotta love the enthusiasm."

"Seriously. I needed that little bit of sunshine." Cambria looked at the sign on the wall in front of her. Gold, three-dimensional block letters read "Elmer Memorial Inpatient Cardiac Center," and beneath it were color-coded boxes, with numbers and small arrows indicating the positioning of the rooms along the floor. "It's this way."

They walked down the corridor, passing a nurses' station and several doors that all looked the same. The floor was relatively quiet, save for the beeps and blips of various medical equipment, and the radio playing on the desk at the nurses' station. Soon they came to an open door with a small plastic sign next to it, bearing the number 517.

As they approached, Blaine walked out, stopping in his tracks when he saw them. "Cambria? What are you doing here?"

"Hey, man." She gave Blaine a short hug. "I got a text from Miles about your dad, and I wanted to check up on you all."

He returned the hug, giving her a soft squeeze. "That's so sweet of you."

"How's Mr. Woodson doing?" She stepped back and looked into Blaine's face.

His expression drawn, he wore his exhaustion on his face. "He's asleep now. The doctors think he may have had a heart attack."

"Yikes," Greg said. "Sorry to hear that, B."

"It's been one hell of a night, I'll tell you that." Blaine ran a hand over his head. "Right now they just want him to rest. They'll run more tests tomorrow."

"What about Miles? Is he in the room?" Cambria asked, resisting the urge to take a peek in the room.

"No, but he's still on hospital property. I can see the side parking lot from the window inside the room, and his car's still here." He touched her shoulder. "He's not taking any of this very well, I'm afraid."

She felt her brow furrow. "Sounds like there's a lot going on…but I'll just ask him and let him reveal as much as he's comfortable sharing."

Blaine nodded. "Well, good luck finding him. I've gotta get back in there."

"Okay. I hope things turn out well." She watched him disappear into the room, then turned to Greg. "I need to find him."

Greg offered a solemn nod. "I'm with you."

The two of them spent time searching the entire cardiac floor, before moving on to the lobby, cafeteria and common areas on the first floor. Finally, Cambria spotted him sitting on a bench in the courtyard between the cafeteria and the staff parking garage. His form, illuminated by the streetlight overhead, appeared closed off, slumped.

Wordlessly, she told Greg to stay put. While he kept watch through the glass pane of the automatic doors, Cambria slipped out into the cool evening air and crossed the brick pathway to where Miles sat.

He reclined sideways on the bench, with one leg stretched out across the seat and his arm draped over the back. His black slacks, wrinkled from his odd positioning, were visible beneath a smart brown trench coat. His face was partially obscured by the brim of the brown fedora pulled low over his brow.

He swiveled his neck to look at her, allowing her a view of his face. "Cambria? What…what are you doing here?" His tone held a mixture of confusion and surprise, but his expression mirrored the stress and tiredness she'd seen displayed on his older brother.

"I wanted to see how your father was doing." She

took a step closer. "And I wanted to know if you were okay, too."

"Is this how you normally treat your 'distractions'?"

She chuckled. "No, but it doesn't matter. I'm here, so tell me, how are you holding up?"

He sighed. "How much time do you have?"

"As much as you need."

He adjusted his positioning, making room for her. Sitting down on the stiff wooden slats next to him, she eased her body close to his. Placing a gentle hand on his thigh, she said, "I'm listening."

Miles stared into Cambria's sparkling eyes, amazed by the care and sensitivity she demonstrated. "It's a long and messy story. Are you sure you want to hear it?"

A soft smile tilted her lips. "I want to hear as much as you feel comfortable telling me, Miles."

He quickly glanced at her casual attire, and the messy curls trying to escape the confines of her black hoodie. It was the least put together he'd ever seen her look. "Did you rush over here? I don't think it's been two hours since I sent you that text."

Her hand went to his forearm, and she gave it a gentle squeeze. "When are you gonna stop stalling, and tell me what happened?"

Realizing that she wouldn't be put off much longer, and feeling the urge to release all the feelings pent up inside, he took a deep breath. As he recounted the events of the evening leading up to Caleb's hospitalization, he tried to fill in enough details to inform her without confusing her.

He watched her eyes widening as she discovered the layers of the Woodson family's current drama, and when he finished, she slowly shook her head. "Wow. I see why you're sitting out here like this. That's…a lot."

"You're telling me. Not only is my family shattered, but so is my image of the kind of man I thought my father was." He dragged his palm over his face. "I don't know what to do with any of this."

Her tone sympathetic, she said, "Do you know where your mother and sisters ended up going?"

He nodded. "Nia texted me. Said Mom is moving into her guest room for the time being, and they're going to send Teagan back over to the house to get some of her stuff."

She cringed. "She moved out, then." Giving his thigh another squeeze, she added, "I'm so sorry you're going through all of this."

He felt his chest rise and fall in time with his deep sigh. "I don't know what's worse—my own pain, or my mother's. She's given her all to this family. I can't even fathom the betrayal she must be feeling right now."

"That sounds really tough." She moved her hand off his thigh, letting it graze across his chest. Heat from her hand permeated the layers of fabric, searing his skin beneath. "At a time like this, though, you have to focus on what's going to make you feel more settled."

He shook his head. "No, I can't. I should be upstairs, getting information from the medical team."

"I just came from your dad's room. He's sleeping, and there's no news except their plans to run more tests tomorrow."

He straightened in his seat. "What about Mom? She's probably…"

She held up her hand. "Hold on. You're going off the rails again. Like I said, you've got to take care of your own well-being. You won't be any help to your parents, or anyone else, if you don't." She sighed. "Trust me. I know this from personal experience."

"Really?" His brow hitched. "The world-famous, multitalented Cambria Harding has a weakness?" He stared in mock disbelief.

She punched him in the shoulder. "Yes, several, actually. Before I came here to vacation, I noticed the way I was feeling, and how it affected the team."

He eyed her for a moment, reading her expression for any sign of exaggeration. Seeing none, he said, "Okay, I'll bite. What happened?"

"The way I interacted with everyone in my touring party changed. There I was, over-rehearsing my dancers, yelling at my background singers about the slightest deviation from the notes, being short with my road crew. Hell, I even snapped at Greg."

He chuckled, in spite of his mood. "Yikes. You took aim at Captain Crusher himself? You must have really been on one, shorty."

She nodded, her gaze shifting away from his face to stare at some distant point above. "I was. Once the burnout hit, nobody within a one-mile radius was safe from my funky attitude. That's why I had to take this time off. I have to regroup, so I can be in the right frame of mind. Not just for the team, or the fans. But for myself."

"I think I understand where you're coming from now." He moved his arm from the back of the bench, letting it come to rest around her shoulders.

"Good. So tell me, how do you normally relieve stress?"

"I work out, or go for a run. You know, something to expend a little energy, get the blood pumping and flowing." He found himself staring at her full lips. While there was no gloss there today, probably due to her haste in getting to the hospital, they still looked as soft and tempting as ever.

She sucked in her lower lip, as if she sensed his attention. "So what are you gonna do to get your blood pumping today, then?"

"This." Tightening his hold around her shoulders, he folded her in close to his body and brought their faces level.

"Miles…" Her voice a breathy whisper, her sultry eyes locked with his, she leaned into him.

A moment later, his lips captured hers. The chill of the evening air fell away, giving way to the heat generated by the closeness of their bodies and the thrill of her kiss. Her lips parted, allowing his tongue to search the warmth of her mouth in all the ways he craved. Her soft purr only spurred him to pull her into his lap and deepen the kiss.

Her hands toured his shoulders and upper arms, making lazy circles that soothed the tension gathered there. He sucked her bottom lip gently into his mouth, sweeping his tongue over its petallike softness, eliciting another purr from her throat.

"Yo." A deep voice resounded nearby.

Drawn out of the moment, Miles drew away from Cambria…only to find her burly bodyguard standing over them.

She blinked several times. "Greg, what…"

"Now, you know I don't interfere in this type of thing normally," Greg said, his voice low. "But since y'all are starting to draw an audience, I thought I'd better make an exception."

"Audience?" Cambria slid off Miles's lap, her eyes darting around. "Oh, snap."

Miles looked for himself, and cringed when he saw the dozen or so people lined up in the cafeteria, watching them through the floor-to-ceiling windows. "Well, shit."

"Do you think they can see me well enough to know who I am?" She looked up to her bodyguard as she posed the question.

He shrugged. "I don't know. I mean, y'all are directly under a streetlamp." He paused. "All I know is, one guy saw me standing at the door and decided to join me. He kept chatting, even though I didn't respond and made it obvious I wasn't interested in making conversation. Then other people started walking up and chatting with him. Mr. Chatterbox noticed y'all out here, and, well…" He jerked his head toward the cafeteria. "Now you've got yourself an audience, complete with commentary."

She stood. "Yeah, so…let's go."

Miles stood, as well. "Where to?"

"My place." She turned to Greg. "Pull the truck around to the lower level of the staff deck. Miles will walk me over there."

His brow furrowed. "Are you sure?"

"Yes."

Miles took Cambria's hand in his. "I'll take good care of her."

Greg didn't look terribly convinced, but offered a short nod to his boss before walking away.

The small crowd in the window began to disband as Miles led Cambria toward the parking deck. "Do you think any of them actually recognized who you are?"

She shook her head. "Nah. If they had, they wouldn't just be hanging out inside like that. Plus there'd probably be at least one overzealous photog here, trying to snap a pic."

As they entered the deck, the familiar black SUV pulled up alongside them. Miles opened the rear passenger door, allowing her to enter first, then stepping in behind her and closing the door.

Ten

At the front door to her condo, Cambria used her electronic fob to disengage the lock. Miles, standing behind her, draped an arm loosely around her waist. "How often do you give your bodyguard the night off so you can have…distractions?"

"Not often enough," she answered with a wry chuckle.

He released her, following her inside and waiting as she closed and locked the door. "We'll make up for lost time tonight, then."

She shook her head, taking off her hoodie and hanging it on one of the hooks by her door, revealing the black camisole she'd thrown on beneath it. "Cool your jets, playboy. I've got something to show you."

He cocked his head to one side. "I like the sound of that."

Grabbing his hand, she led him deeper into her abode, taking him down the hall past her bedroom and the theater room to the last door on the left. "It's in here."

"Lead the way," he said, leaning in to nuzzle her neck.

She opened the door, flipped on the lights and ushered him inside. "Welcome to my private in-home studio."

He joined her in the outer portion of the room, which was set up as a sitting area. A brown leather love seat rested against one wall, flanked by two potted ficus plants. Across from it was the counter holding her recording equipment.

He scratched his chin. "Hmm. There's something very familiar about this room, even though I've never been in it before."

She nodded. "I know. I had it set up to look like the little studio I first recorded in, when I was at Against the Grain." She sighed, thinking back on that magical time, when her dreams were fresh and boundless. "I still miss singing with Eden and Ainsley... This reminds me of those days."

She walked over to the counter, and he trailed her. As she bent over the controls, he entered her space, placing his body flush against her from behind. The slight bulge in his slacks indicated his desire.

"I can barely contain my excitement at being here with you, Cambria."

"I know. Your excitement is currently jabbing me in my back." She turned on the panel, watching as the buttons lit up. "I want to play something for you."

"Okay."

She started an instrumental track playing, the sound filling the space. "A producer sent it to me several weeks ago. It's definitely in my wheelhouse… alternative R&B feel, a hundred and forty-four beats per minute, drums on point. But I just hadn't been able to come up with any lyrics."

"Writer's block?" He gave her a gentle squeeze around the waist.

"You could say that." She turned in his arms, facing him. "I know you probably think the timing is terrible, but inspiration isn't something you can plan. I think I finally have some lyrics in mind."

"So you wanna write 'em down, or…" He watched her, waiting for her answer.

"I wanna sing them. Commit them to digital memory. I'm cool as long as I get a decent draft. The production team can clean it up later."

He inhaled deeply, his eyes closing for a brief moment before opening again. "If I said I wasn't impatient to make love to you, I'd be lying. But I'm not going to rush you. So my only question is, how can I help?"

"Do you know how to work this thing?" She gestured to her sound panel.

He scratched his head. "Probably. I've seen Teagan do it hundreds of times." He released his hold on her and strolled to the counter. Dropping into the chair, he slid up to the panel and pushed a button, pausing the track loop. "I can figure it out. Go on in the booth and let's do this."

She smiled. "Thank you." A few moments later, she was in the sound booth, headphones on, giving him the thumbs-up to restart the track.

As the music filled her ears, she let a few bars of it play before she started singing. The lyrics, which had come to her while she and Miles had been kissing under the streetlamp, were about vulnerability and letting someone in.

As she sang, she kept her eyes closed, allowing the emotions to take over. Each word was infused with feeling, and when she finished, she opened her eyes to find Miles staring at her through the glass partition.

She hung up her headphones and left the booth. An unspoken flicker of desire passed between them, and she jerked her head toward the love seat, walking past him to take a seat there.

By the time her body began to sink into the buttery leather, he was next to her. His arms wound around her and he drew her in for a kiss.

Their tongues mated and danced, the temperature in the room seeming to climb. Emboldened by privacy and by the fire burning inside her, she moved atop his lap, straddling him, without breaking the kiss.

His big hands moved up and down her bare arms, the warmth of his palms causing goose bumps to rise on her skin. He grabbed the tail of her tank and tugged it upward. She broke the seal of their lips long enough to allow him to snatch it off over her head.

He buried his face between her breasts, hands cupping them within the confines of her black lace bra. He inhaled deeply and growled. "You smell like heaven."

She opened her mouth to reply, but the words dissolved as he began palming her breasts, lifting them up above the lacy material. She sucked in a breath as his mouth closed around one hard nipple, while his sure hands undid the clasp behind her. Her hips began to move of their own accord, grinding against his hardness as his hot mouth sucked and teased her nipples.

She flattened her hand against his chest, pushing him back. Snatching the shirt from the center point, she thrilled at the sound of buttons striking the hardwood floor. Then she spread open the halves and tugged down his white tank before leaning in, her mouth connecting to the side of his strong throat.

"Cambria," he growled, his hand coming to the back of her head and weaving its way into the depth of her curls.

She pulled away only after she'd left a bright red mark on the side of his neck. Staring into his hooded eyes, she licked her lips.

"We need to take this to the bedroom," he said gruffly. "If we don't you're gonna get the full force of my 'distraction' right here on this couch."

"You talking big shit right now." Wriggling off his lap, she stood and offered her hand. "Let's see you back it up."

Miles felt his blood rushing to his lower extremities as he gently nudged Cambria back onto her bed.

Once he'd shrugged out of his ruined shirt, his socks and slacks, he joined her there, amazed by the softness of the bedcoverings. Still, they had nothing on the silkiness of her skin.

Propped against the wealth of throw pillows at the head of the bed, she gestured to him with a crooked finger.

Her challenge still echoing in his mind, he closed the space between them, hovering over her. He let his hands roam her upper body while he kissed her lips. Then he trailed his kisses lower, into the crook of her graceful neck, loving the way she sighed in response. Grazing his palms over her nipples, he found them hard and pleading, drawing the attention of his mouth once again. Her hand caressed the back of his neck as he licked and sucked the two dark berries.

Hard seemed too subtle a word to describe his dick as his arousal climbed to near painful level.

He continued moving his attentions lower, noticing the way she tensed when he languished kisses over her abdomen. "Don't tell me you gettin' nervous. A minute ago you wanted me to back up my big shit."

She shivered.

He hooked his fingertips under the waistband of her sweats and panties, dragging them both down. As he tossed the garments away and eased her thighs apart, he heard her whisper his name.

"Hmm?" He hummed into her inner thigh.

"Go…slow…"

"Don't worry, baby. I will." Fully determined to

savor every bit of sweetness she could give, he leaned into her mound and swept his tongue through her folds.

She shuddered, a broken moan slipping from her lips. It was followed by more moans and soft cries as he enjoyed her. He suckled, he licked, he teased, inhaling the aroma of her arousal and enjoying the sounds and sights of her pleasure. When he slipped his index finger inside her wetness, she cursed.

Only when orgasm tore the screams from her lips did he ease away, palms resting on her trembling thighs. Looking down at her in the dim glow of her bedside lamp, he smiled. "You're beautiful when you're cumming."

She drew a deep, shaky breath before uttering two words. "Condom…now."

He left the bed to grab the one in the pocket of his slacks. Stripping off his tank and boxers, he sheathed himself before returning to the bed. Kneeling over her, he took in the sight of her: her passion-hooded eyes, her breasts pushed up by the disheveled bra, her splayed thighs. His dick pulsed with need for her.

She reached for him, grabbing his waist. Shifting his body to the side, she moved from beneath him. "Not like this, Miles."

Hearing her throaty whisper, he followed her lead as she pushed him over onto his back.

Straddling him, she leaned low over him, her breasts dangling in his face. "I wanna ride." A moment later, she lowered herself onto him, enveloping his hardness within her creamy softness.

He gritted his teeth as her tightness threatened to overwhelm him. She was still for a moment, as if taking time to adjust to the feeling of having him inside. Then she began to rock her hips with a slow certainty that curled his toes and sent his soul to heaven.

He grasped handfuls of her round, full hips and held on as she took him for the ride of his life. Through heavy lids, he watched the subtle bounce of her breasts with each movement of her body. He heard the raspy growls coming from his own throat, barely recognizing them.

She was too tight, too hot, too tempting. He'd never had a woman take control this way, never experienced this level of throat-clenching, mind-bending pleasure.

He looked up into her eyes, and she smiled so wickedly he feared she could read his mind. Tossing her head back, those beautiful curls flying around her head like a dark halo, she picked up the pace, rocking her hips faster, harder.

He groaned, low and long.

Completion was coming, and he would not be able to hold it off long.

Again, she seemed to see straight through him, into his soul. "You gonna cum, baby?"

He gasped.

She increased her pace again, purring her pleasure. "Don't…hold…back…on me, Miles."

His body gave in then, to her command, to her tightness, to the ecstasy she gave, and he shouted as he spilled his seed.

She remained atop him, lying down so that her head rested on his chest. After a few moments of silence, while he tried to catch his breath, she asked, "Round Two?"

He grabbed her face and kissed her on the lips. "You wicked, wicked woman."

And all through the night, she showed him just how wicked she could be.

Eleven

The shrill ring of an alarm clock filled Cambria's ears, awakening her. As she opened her eyes and blinked against the assault of bright sunlight, she searched for the source of the sound.

Behind her, she heard Miles grumble under his breath, and felt the bed move as he fumbled around. Moments later, the sound ceased, and his big arm draped over her waist. Drawing her nude body close to his, he kissed the side of her neck. "Sorry about that. I need an obnoxious alarm or else I'll sleep right through it." His voice was deep and thick with the remnants of sleep.

"Noted." She took a moment to enjoy the feeling of waking up with him, of having the warmth of his body against her inside the cocoon of bed linens.

When she'd awakened yesterday morning, she hadn't expected today to begin this way. But, at least for the moment, a sense of contentment settled inside her.

"So, how are you feeling?" He gave her a squeeze. "Did I give you what you needed?"

She swallowed as memories of last night rolled over her like a wave. *You gave me way more than that.* He'd taken her to places she'd never been before, heights of frenzy and passion she'd never imagined. Not wanting to overfeed his ego, she said, "Yes, you did."

"Good." He kissed her neck again, then eased away from her and got up.

The loss of his body heat sent a chill through her, and she tightened the covers around herself, watching him as he walked around the bed to retrieve his scattered clothing. His nude body, bathed in morning light, tempted her to draw him back into bed. He was a well-built man, lean yet muscular.

Stepping into his underwear and slacks, he said, "It pains me to leave those soft curves, believe me. But I need to get back to the hospital to check on Dad."

She stuck her hand up and waved it, dismissing his words. "I totally understand. Please let me know if there's anything I can do for you or the family."

Mostly dressed now, he shrugged into his button-down, then chuckled when he tried to button it. "Oh, shit. Forgot about that." He took it off and tossed it onto her window seat.

She felt embarrassment rise as she was reminded of her actions. "Sorry about that."

He shook his head. "Don't apologize. It was incredibly sexy. Lucky for me, I took my grandma's advice to always wear an undershirt, plus I've got a couple clean T-shirts in my car." He came back to the bed, bent down and kissed her softly on the lips. "I appreciate you, Cambria. You helped break me out of a really bad mood."

She smiled. "Oh, I got a little something out of it, too." She winked. Grabbing her phone, she texted Greg. "Greg will be here any minute. He'll give you a lift back to the hospital."

"That means I better get my kisses in now, then." He dived back into the bed and raised the covers.

He soon smothered her squeal of laughter with his lips.

Later, at the sound of Greg's knock on the door, she drew away. Stroking his cheek, she said, "I'll see you later, Miles."

"Bye, baby." He left her in bed, lingering at her bedroom door for a moment, before slipping out.

She lay there for a little while, savoring the quiet and the last remnants of his woodsy cologne clinging to her bedclothes. Then she got up to begin her day.

She dressed in a pair of jeans, a red turtleneck and matching red sneakers. Tying a red scarf around her hair, she deemed herself fit for public consumption, or at least for today's plans: spending quality time with her aunt and grandmother.

After whipping up a late breakfast of hash browns,

eggs and a croissant with a cup of hot tea, Greg drove her to her grandmother's place.

Lisa brought out the UNO cards, and the three of them sat around the kitchen table for a spirited game.

"Man, it's been forever since I played this." Cambria fanned out her cards in one hand, perusing them.

"Are you just making conversation, Sugar Plum?" Pearl studied her own cards. "Or is that a plea for mercy?"

"Mama!" Lisa laughed. "You're too much."

Cambria chuckled. "Just making conversation, Granny. Besides, I know you don't do mercy when it comes to card games."

"I'm glad you remembered that," Pearl said as she picked up her glass of sweet tea and took a long sip.

"All right, you two." Lisa flipped the top card on the deck. "Looks like the color is red, ladies." She laid down a four, then reached for the bowl of popcorn between her and her niece. "Your turn, Mama."

Pearl eyed her cards for a few silent moments, then slapped down three cards in rapid succession. "The color is now green. Go ahead and draw eight, Sugar Plum."

"Sheesh." Lisa shook her head.

Cambria cringed. Granny had always been savage at the card table, and apparently today would be no different.

While Pearl proceeded to beat the pants off both her youngest child and her granddaughter, conversation flowed easily between the three women.

As Lisa shuffled the cards between hands, she

asked, "So, Cambria. Did you ever pursue that… hobby…we talked about?"

Midsip from her glass of water, Cambria coughed. *Guess Granny's not the only one who doesn't hold back*. "Yes, Auntie. I tried it out."

Lisa's brow hitched as she took her turn, throwing down a blue number eight. "And how did you like it?"

Cambria sucked in her lower lip, trying not to laugh. She knew this was her aunt's clever way of satisfying her curiosity about Miles as a lover without upsetting Granny. Still, she couldn't shake her amusement. "I liked it a lot. I'll probably make a regular thing of it, at least while I'm on vacation."

"Good." Lisa's smile reinforced her approval.

"It's always nice when you discover something you enjoy," Pearl added sagely.

Lisa wasn't as good at hiding her mirth, because she snorted a laugh. "You're absolutely right, Mama." She took a deep breath, as if trying to settle herself, before turning to her niece. "Oh, and I'm gonna let you help me out. Since you were open enough to take my advice, I'll take yours, as well."

Cambria smiled. "I'm glad to hear it."

Pearl slapped down four cards in a row. "The color is yellow. Now draw twelve."

With a sigh, Cambria reached for the pile on the table and drew the dozen cards. She'd just crammed the last one into her deck when her phone went off. She checked the screen and saw a text alert from her accountant, letting her know the latest statement was available. After Granny Pearl embarrassed her for three more rounds of UNO, Cambria set her cards down. "I'm out. I think my dignity and pride have been sufficiently beaten."

"Me, too." Lisa tossed her cards on the pile.

"You two are just sore losers. But, I suppose the game's over, then." Pearl turned sideways in her chair. "Lisa, bring me my walking stick, please."

As Lisa escorted Pearl back to the sewing room, Cambria opened her cloud storage app and accessed her new statement. She didn't really have a head for numbers sometimes, and would be the first to admit that. But there was something different about the figures on this statement: something was off.

So, taking her phone into the living room, she took a seat next to Greg on the plastic-covered sofa and placed a phone call to the one person she thought could help.

Seated in the stiff, vinyl-covered chair at his father's bedside, Miles was jarred from his nap by the ringing of his phone. He searched around, finding it in a crevice between his thigh and the armrest. Swiping the screen, he answered. "Hello?"

"Hi, Miles. It's Cambria."

He swallowed. "Hey there." He hadn't expected to hear from her, at least not so soon. It had only been a few hours since he'd left her house. "What's up?"

"I told you earlier I'd check in on your dad today, remember?" She paused. "How is he? Any news?"

He felt his chest contract. *There she goes, being*

sweet and caring again. Has she forgotten what we're supposed to be doing? "He had a mild heart attack, and he'll need to stay here at least a couple of days to recuperate before they send him home." He glanced over at his father, who was lying in bed watching *In the Heat of the Night.* "He's awake now, watching TV."

"That's good. Sounds like he's out of the woods."

"He is, as long as he follows the doctor's orders and keeps his stress levels down."

"Tell that to your mother," Caleb groused from his perch in bed. His sour expression and folded arms made him look like a child in the throes of a tantrum, but Miles had better sense than to tell him that.

"I heard him," she said. "At least he's up and talking, right?"

"Yeah." Miles chuckled. "Let's hope his mood improves right along with his condition."

"Listen, I know you've got a lot going on right now, but can I ask you a favor?"

His brow hitched. Was she about to ask him something practical? Or something cheeky? "What is it?"

"I got a financial statement from my accountant today. I can't tell what the problem is, exactly, but something's off." She paused. "Please don't feel like you have to do it this minute, but if you get some free time, would you mind looking over it?"

He ran a hand over his head. "Can't promise it'll be anytime soon, but I'll take a look. I'll text you my email." He took a few seconds to send off the text.

"Thanks, I appreciate it." She paused. "I know

you have a lot going on, and I don't want to hold you. But it was nice hearing your voice, and I'm glad your dad is improving."

"I really appreciate you being so caring." He drew a deep breath, feeling the stress of his family situation sitting on his shoulders. *How can I tell her that the more caring she is, the more time I wanna spend making love to her?* He touched his temple, where the beginnings of a tension headache were settling in.

"You still there?" she asked.

"Yes. Sorry." He chuckled. "My thoughts got away from me for a moment."

"I think I can guess the general direction your mind went. I may or may not be thinking about last night, too." She giggled. When she spoke again, her words were soft, just above a whisper. "Go take care of your dad, Miles." Then she disconnected the call.

Sitting there in that hard chair, Miles tucked his phone away and sighed. *She's right. Duty calls.* Looking at his father, who seemed absorbed in the events playing out on the television screen, gave him some sense of calm. *If he's that focused on whatever Detective Tibbs is saying, he must be feeling okay.*

A knock sounded at the door, and it swung open. Blaine stood in the doorway. "It's twelve thirty, bro. My shift."

Miles stood, stretched. "Guess I'll grab a quick lunch before I head to the office."

"I'd skip the hospital cafeteria if I were you," Blaine advised with a shake of his head.

"Got it." He circled around the foot of the bed and headed toward the door. "How's Eden?"

A smile came over his brother's face. "She's doing a lot better now that she's past the morning sickness stage."

"Great." Miles didn't know if he'd ever be a father himself, but he felt a certain degree of excitement about becoming an uncle. "Later, bro." He turned toward Caleb. "I'll see you later, Dad."

His father grumbled a goodbye without looking away from the TV screen.

Miles then slipped from the room and walked to his car. While he drove across town to the 404 building, he turned over in his mind the less-than-ideal ending of his time with Cambria. *It sucks that I had to rush off the way I did. I really wanted to stay with her.*

His mind replayed their lovemaking from the previous night. She'd been so passionate, so vocal, so damn sexy. The sights and sounds of her, the feel of her silken skin, the way she trembled beneath his touch. Being with her had awakened something in him, something he didn't think he could lock away now that it had been released.

He tried to push those thoughts away as he pulled into the drive-through of a local fast-food spot for a burger, fries and a soda. Arriving at work, he took his food upstairs to his office and shut the door behind him.

While he ate, he turned on his computer. Since he'd taken the morning off to be at his father's bedside, he knew there would be plenty of emails and

tasks for him to catch up on. He opened his inbox
and spotted the email from Cambria right at the top.

He slurped the last of his soda. *I may as well take
a quick look at it. Once I get started on work, there's
no telling when I'll get back around to it.* After reading the brief message, he opened the attachment.

It only took a few minutes of perusal before he realized the report was doctored. What made it so bad
was that the person responsible for the forgery hadn't
even done that good a job. He shook his head as he
closed the report and typed a brief reply to Cambria's
email, recommending she get her legal counsel to
evaluate her accountant's books. With that done, he
moved on to the other messages, tackling those that
were important and deleting those that weren't. After
emails he moved on to his other work.

While grabbing a bottle of water from his in-
office mini-fridge, he thought for a moment about
what he'd seen in the financial report. It made him
wonder how deep the rabbit hole of shady dealings
went. How long had this person been taking advantage of Cambria, and at what cost? Worst of all, had
she ever stopped to consider that this person might
be swindling her? This lined up with the old image
he'd had of Cambria as image-centric, self-obsessed
and blissfully unaware of the things that really mat-
tered. Part of him wanted to deal with the person
doing her wrong, and part of him wanted to chastise
her for not looking into this sooner.

He took a swig from the water bottle and returned
to his desk. He thought back on their earlier conver-

sation, and her subtle dismissal. She hadn't laughed, or hung up on him, or said anything hurtful. Actually, her words had been reasonable, a soft-spoken, gentle reminder to return his attention to the more pressing matters at hand.

Yet it still stung, because it wasn't the response he'd really wanted. He felt like a teenager, eager to sit on the phone and listen to her talk about any- and everything. But they both had other things to take care of; she'd simply reminded him of that. Logic told him he shouldn't be disappointed.

But logic didn't offer any comfort now.

Setting aside his complaints, he turned his attention back to the work at hand.

After all, it's work now, play later.

Twelve

"Ms. Harding?"

Cambria looked up from her phone and at the young girl in front of her. "Yes, Brandy?"

"I really want to sing one of your songs for the talent show. Would that be all right?"

She felt the smile tug her lips. "I'm super flattered, Brandy. But I'm afraid it's against the rules to sing any of my songs. Since I'm acting as a judge, it can't look like I'm showing favoritism to any of the competitors. Does that make sense?"

She nodded "Sort of." She looked thoughtful for a moment. "I do have a Janet Jackson song that's my second choice. Maybe I'll sing that instead."

"Can't go wrong with Ms. Jackson. She's a legend."

Seemingly satisfied, Brandy thanked her and walked away.

Cambria returned her attention to her phone's screen. It was Monday evening, and even though it was well after business hours, she'd been texting back and forth with her lawyer. After receiving Miles's email and the advice it contained, she wanted to have her attorney evaluate Harley's records. *Getting good-quality care for Granny isn't gonna be cheap. So if I'm owed any money, I plan to collect.*

Once she'd gotten the confirmation of her lawyer's pending review, she set her phone down on the table and began watching the kids in Miles's self-defense class. They were scattered around the multipurpose room, working on their various acts for the talent show. In order to increase the number of acts, Miles had opened participation to all kids in the neighborhood, so there were quite a few new faces present tonight.

Some of the youngsters were working on a song or dance; one was doing a martial arts demonstration. Another seemed to be working on a piece of spoken-word poetry. Looking around the space at all the youthful energy and creativity on display, she knew the show would be a great one.

A few of the parents were present as well, lined up in folding chairs along the opposite wall from her, observing the practice. Their smiles mirrored her own. *Look at them. Every one of them a unique and talented soul, every one of them somebody's baby.*

Her heart squeezed in her chest at that thought,

and she wondered if she'd ever have a child of her own. When she looked back on her own childhood and the time she'd spent with her parents, she often found the memories less than pleasant. Sure, they'd loved her and met her basic needs. But they'd never seemed to *like* her. Every choice she tried to make seemed to go against what they wanted for her. She'd been an adventurous, free-spirited child, trapped in an ultraconservative home. Her experiences with her parents had limited and stifled her in ways she still struggled with.

Thankfully, Granny Pearl had provided her an alternative—a safe home where she'd felt much freer to be herself.

"What's on your mind?"

The sound of Miles's voice drew her out of her own head and back to reality. He stood in front of the table, wearing a pair of khakis with a powder blue button-down shirt and a pair of caramel loafers.

She wondered if he suspected she might be second-guessing the intimacy they'd shared. His expression now didn't indicate any negative emotion, so she left it alone. *I won't address it unless he brings it up.* Glancing up into his face, she answered his question truthfully. "Just thinking about how much I love my grandmother."

"That's sweet." He moved around the table and sat down in the seat next to her. Tucking his large hands into the pockets of his khakis, he said, "You know, I feel like you know a lot about my family, especially considering all the recent drama you've been privy to. But I can't say I know much about yours."

"Fair enough." She shifted a bit in her chair, facing him. "What do you want to know?"

"I know your grandmother and aunt are here, and that Atlanta is your second home." He paused, watching her intently. "Tell me about your actual hometown, and your parents."

She took a deep breath. "Okay. My parents are named Coletta and Paul, and I grew up in Reno, Nevada."

He nodded. "I know. But those are things I could find out with a quick internet search. I want to know something about your life before you moved to Atlanta."

She swallowed. "Let's see. It gets really hot in Reno, but there's no humidity to speak of. I spent my summers at a female-only Bible camp, and my parents sent me to a private all-girls school. I never even spoke to a boy until after I moved in with my grandmother."

He appeared confused. "What? Why not?"

"My parents wouldn't allow it. They said me talking to boys, even on a friendly level, would only lead to 'sinful behavior.'"

"Wow." He whistled. "They sound pretty damn tough."

"They were. That's why I'm so grateful to Granny for letting me come live with her when I started high school." She sighed. "I had to get out of there—it was so oppressive at home."

"I can sort of hear that longing for freedom when I listen to your early solo music."

She felt her brow hitch. "You've listened to my early work?"

He nodded. "Sure, I have. *Among the Stars* is a great album."

She smiled at the mention of her debut release. "That album was incredibly personal. It's gratifying to hear you praise it like that."

"I call them as I see them." He paused, his gaze resting on his students. "It's amazing the ways our family life shapes so much of who we are." He scratched his chin. "I hope this isn't weird of me to say, but I feel a little bit better about what's going on with my parents, now that I've heard about yours."

She shrugged. "Nah. I get it." She gave his shoulder a gentle nudge. "I heard your dad's improving a lot."

He nodded. "Yes. He's gonna get to go home soon, we hope." He paused. "He doesn't want to stay in the hospital any longer, but isn't looking forward to going home to an empty house, either. My mom is still staying at Nia's."

"That must be hard. Not just on him, but on the whole family. I hope things settle out soon."

He ran a hand over his close-trimmed curls. "Right now, I'm just clinging to my hope that they can come back from this."

They both fell silent for a short time, each of them keeping their own counsel as they watched the kids rehearse their acts.

A woman in a pink tracksuit approached the table, a bright smile on her face. "Hi, Ms. Harding. I'm so pleased you took time out to come and help our kids. As a mother, I really appreciate it."

"That's really great to hear." She stood, shook the woman's hand. "I'm happy to do it."

"I don't want to hold you up. But let me tell you how much I love your music, and how much I miss SWATZ Girls!" She placed a hand over her chest. "They just don't have any good girl groups anymore," she lamented before walking away with a wave.

Sitting back down in her seat, Cambria considered the woman's words. "She's right, you know. Girl groups are rare nowadays."

"Yeah. I always chalked it up to ego," Miles surmised, stroking his chin. "Everybody wants to sing lead, be the star."

She cringed. "Is that how you think of me? You think my ego made me leave my friends behind?"

He shook his head. "No, that's just a general statement. I don't know your personal reasons and circumstances."

She didn't find his answer all that convincing, but she let it slide, nonetheless. The more she thought about Eden and Ainsley, and the great times they'd had together, the more she wanted to recapture some of that magic. Snapping her fingers together, she said, "I've got it. I'm gonna try and see if the girls will do a SWATZ Girls reunion with me. One night only, as part of your talent show."

* * *

Miles's ears perked up at Cambria's declaration. "Do you really think you can make that happen? You ladies haven't performed together in years."

She rubbed her hands over her wild curls, smoothing them away from her face. "Honestly, I don't know. But a SWATZ Girls reunion would be so awesome and so epic that I'm willing to give it a shot."

He nodded. "I agree, it would be pretty epic. ATLians would come from far and wide to witness it." He checked the time on his phone, his eyes widening. Dang, class should have gotten out ten minutes ago. Standing, he added, "If you can make it happen, I know tickets will sell out, and fast."

He started walking toward the front of the room, where the inspirational posters featuring Black luminaries like Gwendolyn Brooks, Malcom X and Tupac were tacked to the cement walls. Clapping his hands together, he called out, "Attention, please." Once the room quieted, he said, "Y'all have been working so hard you've gone over class time. I want to thank you all, kids, parents and guardians, for your dedication to making this talent show a success."

"Thank you, Mr. Woodson," a parent called out.

He smiled. "You know I love this community, so it's my honor. Now go ahead and wrap up, gather your belongings, and I'll see you back here Wednesday for the next rehearsal."

He watched as everyone began putting away various equipment and props, then began retrieving their book bags and other items from the wall hooks inside the storage area that connected to the multi-purpose room.

Yet among all the activity happening around him, nothing stood out more to him than Cambria. He watched as she rose, strolling across the room to meet up with her bodyguard. His hungry eyes savored the view of her shapely ass and thick thighs in the black leather pants she wore.

Arriving by Greg's side, Cambria tapped him on the shoulder. Holding up her phone, she showed him something on the screen and they both laughed. A twinge of jealousy tugged at Miles's psyche. He wanted to be the one sharing that moment of humor with her. He knew he had no rights or claims to her time and attention, but he felt the twinge all the same.

The room finally emptied out, leaving only the three of them inside. Cambria and Greg's laughter now echoed in the big room, making Miles feel even more left out.

Drawing a deep breath, he walked across the polished hardwood floor, directly to the spot where Cambria and her bodyguard stood. After bumping fists with the former wrestler, he said, "Remind me to get your autograph, Captain Crusher. As far as I'm concerned, you're the real celebrity."

Cambria cocked her brow at his chiding, but her smile remained intact.

Greg laughed again. "Sure thing, man. But you'd better stop teasing my boss lady before she puts you in a half nelson." Shaking his head, Greg walked toward the door and leaned against the frame.

"So I'm assuming you saw my message about your financial statement?" He moved closer to her, still leaving a bit of distance between them. "I meant to ask you about it earlier."

She nodded. "I did, and I already let my lawyer know that she needs to evaluate my accountant's records."

"Will your lawyer be able to do it soon?" He leaned his back against the cement wall. "Because there's some shady stuff going on, and the longer it continues, the more money you stand to lose."

"I know. She's going to go there in person tomorrow and look everything over, page by page."

"That's a relief." He tried to choose his next words carefully, unsure of how she would receive them. "Have you considered studying up on financial matters? Maybe taking an online class or something like that?"

She shook her head. "No, I hadn't considered that. I already have approximately two million things to do on any given day, and I don't think I have the bandwidth to do anything extra."

"I get that you're busy. But all the work you're doing can never really pay off if someone is swindling you, taking advantage of your lack of knowledge for their own selfish gain."

Her smile faded. "Okay, I get it."

"I'm not sure you do. There's no way someone could have gotten away with such blatant trickery as what I saw on that report, if you had educated yourself about…"

KIANNA ALEXANDER   135

She held up her hand. "Okay, cut it. You sound like my dad."

He felt his frustration rise. "Cambria, I'm only trying to…"

"Help me? I know what I need to do. You've made yourself clear, so quit talking to me like I'm an idiot." She turned her back on him and began walking away.

He trailed behind her. "Come on, Cambria. You can't get mad at me for telling you what you need to hear."

"And who says you get to decide what I need, Miles?" She stopped and propped her fist on her hip, the metal rings hanging from her leather jacket jingling in time with her movements. "It's weird how we just met, and yet you've assigned yourself so much power and importance in my life."

He took a step back, shaking his head. "Fine, have it your way. It's up to you to decide if it's important enough to protect your money." Smoothing a hand over his face, he said, "Just let me know if you can work things out with your friends for this group reunion. If you can pull it off, I'll need to update the website, the social media pages and the tickets."

Her lips still pursed tight, she nodded. "Fine. I'll see you later, Miles." A second later, she and her guard exited the room. He could hear the echo of their footsteps on the tile floors of the lobby, then the creak of the main door as they left.

With a sigh, he began walking around the room, tidying up in preparation to leave. How had a simple suggestion, an attempt at giving her advice, turned into an argument? She did ask for his help, after all, when she first sent him the document. Did she really think he was trying to belittle or antagonize her?

Locking up the building and heading to his car, he thought about the two Cambrias he'd met so far. One was talented, vivacious and passionate. The other was suspicious, snappy and defensive.

Who knows how many other sides she has? I'm not sure I should stick around to find out.

Making love with her had been amazing. But if they kept up their little liaison, he knew there would be pain and strife on the horizon.

Thirteen

Standing in her closet, Cambria did a slow turn, taking in her reflection in the full-length mirror on the back wall. The designer bodysuit, fashioned of black silk and lace, hugged every curve. Strategic cutouts at the shoulders, the abdomen and the hips showed off a few of her favorite tattoos. She grinned at her reflection while stepping into a pair of black leather pumps. Grabbing her favorite black trench from the rack next to her, she shrugged into it, tying the waist belt.

Greg looked up from his book as she entered the living room. "Need me to take you somewhere?"

She nodded. "Yes. Drop me at the 404 building, please."

His brow hitched. "I'd ask why…but I like my job."

Chuckling, he closed his book and tucked it beneath his arm. He walked toward the door and opened it for her as he fished the keys to her black SUV out of his pants pocket with his free hand.

Once they were underway, she threw one leg over the other and watched the passing scenery. She thought about texting Miles, but decided against it.

He seems like the type to work late, so I'm 90 percent sure that at six on a Tuesday evening, his office is the best place to catch up with him.

She didn't want him to see her coming, honestly. Mr. Straitlaced-and-Serious could probably use a little excitement in his life, and tonight, she planned to provide it. *I can't wait to see the look on his face when I pull up on him.*

She thought back on their conversation the previous night, and the way he'd condescended to her about her lack of financial savvy. She sighed, remembering how he'd leaned into lecturing her, seeming to take pleasure in calling her out for all the things she didn't know.

As annoyed as she'd been with him, it didn't change her attraction to him. One night together simply wasn't enough. Even as her mind reminded her how his words had made her feel, her body craved his touch, his kiss. So she intended to show up at his office, shut the door behind her, and show him just how much of a distraction she could be.

Greg helped her out of the truck at the front of the 404 building and asked, "Do you want me to wait here in the parking lot?"

She shook her head. "No, but stay close. I'm not sure how long I'll be here."

"Cool. I've got my book. Maybe I'll hit up that little coffee shop up the road." He shut the back door, then climbed back into the driver's seat.

She entered through the main doors and strolled past the reception desk, waving to the woman seated there.

"Ma'am, do you have an appointment?" The receptionist looked at her for a long moment before her eyes widened. "Omigosh! Excuse me, go right ahead, Ms. Harding."

"Thank you." She breezed past the desk and down the corridor toward the elevator bank, following the small signs mounted on the wall.

A petite, caramel-skinned sista stepped out of a room to her left, pausing in the hallway. As Cambria looked at her, she realized she looked familiar. "Hi. Aren't you Teagan?"

She nodded. "I am. Nice to see you, Ms. Harding."

She waved her off. "You can call me Cambria."

"Cool. I'll assume you're here to see my twin?" She folded her arms over her chest, the large, bell-like sleeves of her colorful tunic fluttering over her abdomen.

"I am."

Teagan grinned. "Good. Maybe you can break him out of his foul mood, so I can stop feeling it secondhand." Giving a mock salute as she passed her in the other direction, she added, "He's on the fourth floor, suite B."

"Thanks." Chuckling to herself, she went to the elevator and pressed the up button.

When the car deposited her on the fourth floor a short while later, she went straight to the suite Teagan had indicated, and knocked on the closed door.

A minute later, he swung the door open.

She raked her gaze over him, from his round, surprised eyes to his slightly disheveled look. With the buttons at his throat undone and the ink pen stuck behind his ear, he appeared to have been working hard for an indeterminate length of time.

"Cambria?" Eyes still wide, he asked, "What... what are you doing here?"

"Giving you the break you look like you desperately need." She offered him a sultry smile. "Can I come in? I'd hate to have to call Greg back. He's probably just sitting down to read."

He swallowed, swiped his tongue over his lower lip and stepped back. Gesturing with his hand, he said, "Come on in."

She entered, and he closed the door quietly behind her. Glancing at the piles of papers on his desk, she then glanced back his way. "When were you planning on knocking off for the night, Miles?"

He shrugged. "I've been spending mornings at the hospital with Dad, then coming to work in the afternoon. So...I'm a little behind." He walked behind the desk and sat down in his chair.

She sauntered over to him, untying the belt at her waist as she walked. "Well, me and my outfit say it's time to call it a night." She opened the halves of the coat.

He gasped, then groaned, his eyes greedily drinking her in. "Fuck."

"That's exactly what I had in mind." She took off the coat, tossing it over his guest chair and sitting down in his lap. "I know we disagreed yesterday." She cupped his chin in one hand, inviting him to look into her eyes. "But as far as I can tell, we both need this distraction. Do you agree?"

He nodded, his hands sliding over the soft fabric of her bodysuit. As his palm grazed over her bare hip, he growled, "How do I get this thing off you?"

She giggled. "You don't have to. Just unsnap it."

He growled again and pulled her face to his, capturing her mouth in a passionate kiss. Easing his hand between her parted thighs, he found the snaps and undid them. She moaned into his mouth as he slipped his long fingers beneath the fabric. And when he slid a finger inside her, she purred.

He pulled back from the kiss, but not from touching her. "You're so wet." He licked his lips. "I need to see how sweet you are." He raised his finger to his mouth and sucked it clean.

She shivered. "Mmm."

He shoved a stack of papers aside, patted the cleared section of the desktop. "Sit up here for me, baby."

She did as he asked, while he remained in his chair. A heartbeat later, he used his palms to widen her thighs, lowered his chair and leaned forward.

She gripped the back of his head, hands splayed in his curls as he swept his tongue through her folds. When he closed his mouth over her bud and began to suckle gently, she used her hand to stifle a cry of passion. It wasn't long before she came, legs quivering, insides pulsing, and juices running down her thighs to sully his big, fancy desk.

He straightened in his chair, wearing a broad grin. Licking his lips, he said, "You were right. This is just what I needed."

Still trembling, she suddenly became aware of her ringing phone. Squirming off the desk, she grabbed it from the pocket of her trench. Seeing the name on the screen, she said aloud, "It's Eden."

He shrugged. "So what? We're busy." He came over to where she stood, draping an arm around her waist and bringing his lips to the hollow of her neck.

The phone stopped ringing then, and a text came through, also from Eden.

We need to talk. Call me now.

She cringed. "I have to call her back. I've been trying to get a hold of her for weeks now, and this is the first time she's reached out."

He frowned. "Can't it wait?"

"I'm sorry, Miles. It can't, especially if you really want a reunion for your talent show."

He sighed, releasing her. "All right. Do what you gotta do."

"Thanks for understanding." Doing her best to

tamp down her disappointment at not being able to finish their little game, she straightened her clothes, donned her coat and left.

After Cambria slipped out, Miles sat back in his chair, turning it to face the window. He could still smell her arousal, the scent of which filled his office and the sticky remnants of which he'd have to clean off his desktop.

Frustration flowed through him, hot and fast like a pyroclastic flow. He sat in that chair, hard and wanting her, craving to bury himself between her soft thighs, for several more minutes before he finally got up. Using a cleaning wipe to restore his desk to its pre-Cambria state, he reorganized the papers before gathering his things and leaving for the evening.

Driving through the darkness coming toward him, he knew there was no way he'd be able to sleep. His state of mind was too jumbled right now. Unsure of what else to do, he engaged the hands-free calling in his car and called his father's hospital room.

Gage answered the phone. "Hello?"

"Gage, it's Miles. What's Dad up to?"

"Doing a crossword puzzle. Why, what's up?"

"Let me talk to him right quick."

"Okay."

A moment later, Caleb's voice filled the cab of his vehicle. "Miles? It's Dad."

"Hey, Dad. Can I talk to you for a minute?"

"I mean, I'm not going anywhere until they spring

me from this joint, so why not?" He coughed. "What's on your mind, son?"

"It seems I've gotten involved with Cambria Harding."

"It *seems* you have? Or you actually have?"

Miles sighed. "I definitely have. We're not in a relationship or anything like that, but we've been—" he chose his words carefully, trying to push past the awkwardness of talking to his father about sex "—spending time together."

Caleb was quiet for a moment before he said, "I hope you've been wearing protection while you…"

That took the awkwardness level up about ten notches. "Whoa, Dad. Whoa. Yes, I've been using protection."

"Good. So what's the problem, then?"

Miles hesitated. "I…I don't even know. I guess I need advice. I feel like there may be more between us than what we originally intended, and I don't know what to do about it."

A bitter chuckle escaped the older man's lips. "Son, I know you're not asking me for advice about women and relationships. I'm the last person on earth you should be asking about that right now." He paused. "I know. I'll hand the phone back to your brother, ask him."

"Dad, wait!"

"Miles, what have you gotten yourself into?" Gage's voice filled his car.

Miles sighed and recounted what he'd told his

father. "I don't know what to do here. I'm not sure what I feel, what she feels, any of it."

"Well, that sounds unpleasant. But at least you've experienced her." Gage chuckled. "Not many dudes can say that."

He rolled his eyes. "Come on, Gage. This has gone way beyond bragging rights now." He stopped at a red light, and ran his hand over his head. "I'm not gonna lie. I see what you and Blaine have with Ainsley and Eden. Hell, even Teagan is boo'd up with Maxton. That's basically all of us...except Nia."

"Nah. I think we can all agree Nia will probably enter into some kind of civil union with her laptop." Gage laughed. "I love our big sis but she's a workaholic."

"Yeah, she is. She might get there one day, though." He shook his head, wondering what his sisters and his mom might be conversing about right now, since the three Woodson women were most likely together. "The thing is, I never thought I wanted any type of serious relationship. Now I'm not so sure."

"Bro, you gotta hash this out with Cambria." He heard Gage's exhale. "I can't tell you what's going through her mind. Only way to know is to ask her."

"She keeps running from me, man. I'm not even gonna tell you what we just did in my office. But she bolted on me in the middle of it."

Gage whistled. "In the office? So the songbird got you acting up like that, lil bro?"

"Gage, don't play with me right now. I'm not in the mood."

"My bad, bro." He seemed to sober up then, his tone becoming more serious. "Look, I'm sorry. What you're going through sounds rough, and I shouldn't be making light of it. My advice for right now is, fall back. If she really wants you, she won't be able to stay away for too much longer."

He sighed, slowly releasing the breath. "I guess you're right." He turned left at an intersection, then into the parking lot of his townhome development. "I'm about to pull up to my house, so I'll let you go."

"All right. Keep me posted on how it turns out." He lowered his voice. "And I'm gonna need some more details on what exactly y'all was doing in your office."

"Bye, Gage." Shaking his head at his older brother's foolishness, he ended the call. As he pulled into his garage and cut the engine, he thought about Gage's advice to back off, and let Cambria come to him.

She came to me tonight. But she was outta there before the evening could get off the runway. What am I supposed to make of that?

He entered his darkened house through the side door, locking it behind him. He opened the refrigerator, grabbed a bottle of beer and popped the top. Taking a swig, he headed for his living room and dropped onto his dark green leather sofa. He flipped on the television and turned it to the twenty-four-hour sports network, but as the ticker rolled by and the talking heads spouted the stats from today's matchups, he paid scant attention.

Instead, his mind tried to work out his feelings

for Cambria. Was it a fascination? Lustful longing? Or something deeper?

Gage's advice seemed sound, as much as he hated to admit it. There were too many things going on right now: the talent show, their father's ill-health, their parents' marriage imploding, not to mention the scandal of the now confirmed outside child. And beyond that, the company's thirty-fifth anniversary was rapidly approaching. After all the buildup and publicity the marketing team had been doing throughout the year, the city of Atlanta would still expect the Woodsons to put on the social event of the year, regardless of whatever drama they had going on.

He finished up his beer and set the bottle on the coffee table, and fell back against the softness of his sofa. Blowing out a breath, he tried to settle into acceptance as easily as he sank into the cushions.

I gotta back off from this girl. The last thing I need in my life right now is more drama.

Fourteen

As she sat in the private party room inside Cyclades Mediterranean Fare, Cambria found herself nervously tapping her foot. Outside the confines of the room, the restaurant hosted a medium-sized midweek lunch crowd of twenty or so diners. But since both her fame and the nature of the occasion demanded a certain degree of privacy, she'd booked this room in the back, far removed from the folks enjoying a little hummus and falafel before they returned to work or school. Greg, stationed just outside the private room, was tasked with helping the staff ensure that no one other than Eden, Ainsley or their waiters entered the space.

She shifted, glancing out the window behind her. Midtown was in full swing, traffic moving down

I-85 at a snail's pace while the peak of One Atlantic Center rose to kiss a crystal-blue autumn sky. Resting her gaze on a particularly puffy cloud, she wondered what this meal would bring.

I really shouldn't be nervous. These women are some of my oldest friends. Yet she couldn't shake the uneasiness she felt. There were so many years spent apart and so many things unsaid between the three of them that she didn't know how today would go. She'd come here hoping to convince them to reunite, when in actuality, she felt lucky they were even speaking to her at all.

The door to the room opened, drawing her attention. Eden and Ainsley entered, escorted by the waiter. Almost immediately, Cambria's eyes were drawn to the swell of Eden's belly beneath her yellow Empire-waist maxi dress. Ainsley, dressed in black slacks, a teal sweater and black loafers, had her arm linked with her cousin's.

Cambria stood at they approached the table. "Hey, Eden. Ainsley. I'm so glad y'all could meet up with me."

"It was time," Eden admitted as she slid onto the chair diagonal to Cambria.

"Yes. I'm glad you called." Ainsley sat next to Eden, right in front of Cambria.

Sitting down now that they both were seated, Cambria offered a smile. "Feel free to have anything you like."

"Thanks," Eden said. "I'm eating for two and Mediterranean food is about all I'm craving these days."

The waiter approached. "Welcome, ladies. I hung back for a minute to let you three get settled. What drinks can I get for you?" He jotted down their choices of drink and an order of hummus and pita bread as an appetizer, then left with his pad.

"So," Ainsley began, tracing a circle on the white tablecloth with her index finger, "what made you reach out?"

Cambria swallowed. "I've reached out a few times over the last few weeks. As soon as I knew I would be taking some time off, I wanted to let you both know so we could meet up while I was in the city."

"That checks out. But it's been about two weeks since you last called. We thought you'd given up, or changed your mind. Until yesterday." Ainsley stared at her expectantly. "So, what gives? Gotta be some reason."

Cambria balked, aware of the slight accusation in Ainsley's tone. "I stopped reaching out because it didn't seem like y'all were going to respond. I tried again yesterday because I have a favor to ask."

Conversation ceased briefly while the waiter delivered their drinks and the appetizer, then took their food orders. As soon as he disappeared, they picked up where they left off.

"You say you need a favor? From little ol' us? What could the world-famous Cambria Harding possibly need from us?" An edge of bitterness colored Ainsley's tone.

Eden grabbed her cousin's forearm. "Ains, watch yourself. I told you, no bad vibes around the baby."

Ainsley's expression changed then, softening considerably as she patted Eden's belly. "Sorry about that, lil cuz."

Cambria sighed. "Listen, I can't even be upset at the way you're questioning me. All things considered, your caution is warranted."

"I'm glad you know that." Ainsley gave her a little half smile. "We came here because we want to hash this out, once and for all."

"It's not good for the baby for me to hold on to grudges and bad feelings." Eden circled her hand over her belly. "Honestly, it's not good in general."

Drawing a deep breath, Cambria said the words that had been in her heart and mind for many years now. "I'm sorry. When I left the group, I wasn't in the right state of mind. I put myself first, and even though it worked out well for me, I know it was a selfish, inconsiderate decision to make." She paused, feeling the tears gathering in her eyes. "I also know that I'm not owed forgiveness just because I apologized. Either way, I wanted you both to know I'm sorry."

Silence fell over the table, and she could see the two of them weighing out her words. Before long, there were three sets of wet eyes at the table.

"I made my apology. Now I just want to listen. Tell me how my decision affected your lives." Cambria leaned forward, hoping they would see that she was truly interested in what they had to say.

"When you left, we had two very different reactions," Eden admitted. "Ainsley was angry, as you can probably tell. But me, I was mostly hurt."

Cambria swallowed the lump of guilt building in her throat, but said nothing. She'd promised to listen, and no matter how much it hurt to hear these things, her friends deserved the opportunity to speak their truth.

Eden continued, wiping a wayward tear running down her cheek. "It just seemed so sudden. It's not that I don't understand why you took the opportunity. I just wish we'd had some warning, some indication that you were gonna leave us."

"That note you left just didn't cover it." Ainsley shook her head slowly. "It was almost an insult. And then to have Blaine come and explain it to us after the fact, instead of calling us yourself?" She covered her mouth, stifling a sound that was both groan and sob. "How could you?"

The two waiters who placed their food on the table were treated to three sobbing women. As the waitstaff soundlessly moved away and closed them inside the room again, Ainsley started to laugh.

Confused, Cambria sniffled. "What? Why are you laughing?"

"I just realized how weird we must look, crying into our food in a restaurant in the middle of the day." She wiped her tears with a white linen napkin.

"She's right, we look a mess right now." Eden fanned her damp face with both hands. "Tears are healing, right? I guess we've purged our souls."

Cambria's heart pounded in her ears as Ainsley

reached across the table, maneuvering around their plates to grab her hand. "Forgetting what happened will take a long time. But forgiveness? I can give that now."

"Me, too. It's time we move past this." Eden smiled while reaching for Cambria's other hand. "Besides, I miss my friend."

"I've missed you both, too." Cambria squeezed both their hands. "So, so much."

After a few moments, Eden released her friend's hand. "All right. Let's eat before this good food gets cold. The baby's hungry!"

The three of them laughed more before digging into their souvlaki. As Cambria savored the tender chunks of beef and crisp vegetables, she basked in the glow of having her friends back in her life.

When they'd finished their meal and the plates had been cleared away, Ainsley and Eden joined Cambria on her bench seat beneath the window. Draping an arm around each of their shoulders, Cambria said, "About that favor. How would y'all feel about a SWATZ Girls reunion? One night only, for charity."

Ainsley grinned. "I'd love it. It's been way too long since we sang together."

"Get me a stool to sit on and I'm there," Eden said, rubbing her belly. "We're gonna be rusty as hell, though. Probably should rehearse a little."

"Bet." Cambria cleared her throat, and began singing the opening stanza of one of their old songs, "Sweet Like Candy."

Ainsley joined in on tenor, then Eden took her

place on the soprano notes, both their voices blending beautifully with her alto. The two waiters reentered, looking on in awe as the room filled with the sounds of them harmonizing.

Cambria could feel herself smiling as she sang with her two favorite musical partners.

The old magic is still there.

Late Wednesday afternoon, Miles picked up his phone, trying to ascertain why his notifications had suddenly gone wild. Swiping the screen, he chuckled when he saw the video circulating the web.

He watched, awed at the beautiful sound of Cambria, Eden and Ainsley singing one of their old tunes. Their expressions conveying happiness and ease, they ran through the entirety of the short ballad. As they wrapped up, the man recording asked from off camera, "Are y'all getting back together?"

Cambria answered. "One night only, for the 404 Cares Talent Show."

The video ended after that, and he glanced down at the view counter and felt his eyes widen. *Well over forty thousand people had seen the video since it went online about an hour ago.*

His phone continued to ping as he closed the video, but these pings were from the app tied to the ticket vendor site he'd been using to fill seats for the talent show. Opening the app, he felt his eyes bulge for a second time. The show was now sold out, and a quick look at the statistics tabs showed that the two hundred and six remaining tickets had all sold over the last ten minutes.

He felt the grin spread across his face. Cambria's idea for a girl group reunion had paid off, big-time. *Now I'll definitely be able to help those other families on the waiting list. This is amazing.*

She's amazing.

He closed the app and tried to figure out how to configure the chairs in the theater at the community center to meet maximum capacity. Knowing he'd probably need a diagram to do that, he set that thought aside for the moment. For a split second, he contemplated moving to a larger venue to accommodate more attendees. Then he shook his head. *Nah. Nine days just isn't enough time to pull off a big change like that. It would only lead to chaos and confusion.*

He returned to his desk and opened his browser. Once he had a few tabs active, he moved between them, updating the 404 Cares website and all the social media accounts to reflect that tickets to the talent show were officially sold out. Closing the tabs, he opened the spreadsheet with the names of the eleven families on the wait list, cut them and pasted them into the main spreadsheet. It touched his heart to know he could help every single family who'd applied, and he knew he had Cambria to thank for that, at least in part.

He picked up his phone and dialed her number. Instead of ringing as it usually did, the phone went straight to voice mail. A bit perplexed, he tried her one more time, with the same results. Setting the phone down, he went back into his files so he could take a peek at the wish list forms each family had filled out.

His phone buzzed, vibrating the desktop to indicate an incoming text. Glancing at the screen, he saw a message from Cambria.

Can't talk now. Call you later.

He blew out a breath. Had she just sent him a form text? He stared at the phone for a moment, then sat it down. He didn't want to spend time hypothesizing as to what pressing activity she might be involved in that meant she couldn't answer his call. After all, she was in town on vacation. Whatever the case, he couldn't shake the annoyance that she'd dismissed his call.

I've got to stop doing this with her. I can't keep giving her opportunities to reject me, to make me feel small.

This was their first interaction since she'd shown up half-dressed at his office the previous evening, only to end up splayed across his desk. And now she couldn't even be bothered to type out a text.

He turned his attention back to the wish lists, putting his "distraction" out of his mind. He was still reading over one of the forms when his desk phone rang.

"Hello?"

"Hi, am I speaking with Miles Woodson?"

He leaned back in his chair. "Yes, and who is this?"

"My name is Cici Castellano, from…"

"Entertainment Buzz This Week," he said, finishing her statement. He'd seen the nationally syndicated news and gossip program on more than a few occasions. "I'm familiar. What can I do for you?"

"Well, Mr. Woodson, in light of the recent viral videos circulating the internet, I'd just like to ask you a few questions about your upcoming charity event, and Ms. Harding's role in it." She paused. "Can you spare about twenty minutes for an interview?"

He shrugged. "Sure. What do you want to know?"

"Great. So, what can you tell me about your relationship with Cambria Harding?"

He cleared his throat. "I don't know her that well. She's more of a friend of my older brother Blaine. However, I'm very grateful she agreed to participate in my upcoming charity talent show."

"I see. Can you tell us a little bit about your charity, and the event?"

"Sure." This was the whole reason he'd agreed to be interviewed. "I started 404 Cares about eleven years ago, because I saw so much need in the community around me. It was my way of giving back to Greater Atlanta, the place I call home. In terms of the talent show, it will be held in just over a week, and the proceeds will benefit local families by providing food, gifts and warm clothes this holiday season."

"That sounds like a wonderful cause. Can you tell me about Ms. Harding's role in the event?"

"She'll be acting as a celebrity judge, as well as performing with her former girl group mates."

"Is that so? And do you think Ms. Harding's music is appropriate for kids, Mr. Woodson?"

He frowned, not understanding her approach, but answering truthfully anyway. "No, I don't think Cambria's music is child-friendly, but she won't be performing any of her solo songs at the event, so that's of no consequence."

"Hmm." Cici seemed to be considering his words. "Let me take that question one step further. Do you think of Ms. Harding as a proper role model for young African American girls?"

His frown deepened because he sensed some kind of doublespeak foolery afoot. "Being a role model isn't really Cambria's job. That responsibility falls on the parents and other adults in those girls' lives. I'd say the same for all children. Celebrities are entertainers. They aren't meant to be anyone's role model."

"I see." Cici paused. "At any rate, how can people find out more about your charity, and the work you do?"

Glad she'd changed back to the topic of actual importance, he answered, "I'd invite people to purchase tickets for the talent show, but as of about an hour ago, we're all sold out." He paused. "People are welcome to check out our website, Yes404Cares dot com, or follow us on all social platforms at Yes404Cares."

"Thank you so much, Mr. Woodson. I only have one more quick question for you."

"Go right ahead."

"When it comes to the issue of Keegan Woodbine…"

His blood turned to ice at the mention of that name. "No comment."

Cici pressed him for an answer. "Are you sure, Mr. Woodson? The public would love to know your…"

"I won't be commenting on that subject, Cici. You have yourself a good rest of the day." Without waiting for her response, he replaced the phone in the cradle.

Fifteen

Cambria rolled over in bed Thursday morning, opening her bleary eyes to bright sunlight. Sitting up, she stretched before padding to the bathroom.

Freshly showered and dressed in a pair of pink leggings and a tunic-length furry sweater, she stepped into her favorite bunny slippers and headed for the kitchen. She played a little nineties pop on her phone as she whipped up a simple breakfast: scrambled eggs, turkey bacon, and toast with hot tea.

Sitting down at the table with her plate and steaming mug, she folded a leg beneath her. While she ate, she checked her phone. Her brow furrowed as she saw the sixteen notifications she had for text messages and direct messages on various social apps.

They were from her manager, her aunt Lisa, even her hairdresser. And they all said different versions of the same thing.

Have you seen Entertainment Buzz This Week today?

Confused, she responded to her aunt's message.

No, I haven't, Auntie. Everybody keeps asking me that. What's going on?

Her aunt responded right away. They're replaying the segment now, turn on channel 48.

Finishing up the last bit of her breakfast, Cambria carried her mug into the living room and flopped onto the couch. Glancing at Greg, who was reading in the armchair in the corner, she asked, "Have you watched any TV today?"

He shook his head. "Almost finished with this thriller novel. I'm so wrapped up in this I hadn't thought about the TV."

She grabbed the remote from the armrest and turned the TV on, flipping to the channel her aunt indicated.

Onscreen was an olive-skinned, dark-haired woman in a fuchsia jacket, who looked vaguely familiar. The woman smiled as she spoke. "Welcome back to *Entertainment Buzz This Week*. I'm society correspondent Cici Castellano, with an exclusive interview with music mogul and philanthropist Miles Woodson. I caught up with the youngest son of the storied family by phone, to find out more about his upcoming charity event, as well as his personal association with edgy R&B it-girl and recent viral sensation, Cambria Harding. Here is the audio of that interview."

While the television displayed a series of photos of Miles, from various charity events, the audio played over it. The reporter asked questions about 404 Cares, but managed to sprinkle in quite a few questions related specifically to Cambria. She found herself cringing, feeling her own rising ire as she listened to his answers.

"So, what can you tell me about your relationship with Cambria Harding?"

Miles's voice responded, "I don't know her that well. She's more of a friend of my older brother Blaine."

She snorted at that one. *Oh, so he doesn't know me that well? That didn't stop him from having sex with me, did it? Or devouring me like a dessert on top of his desk.*

Cici posed another question on the audio. "And do you think Ms. Harding's music is appropriate for kids, Mr. Woodson?"

"No, I don't think Cambria's music is child-friendly," Miles answered, and Cambria noted that he sounded pretty sure of himself.

"Do you think of Ms. Harding as a proper role model for young African American girls?"

"Celebrities are entertainers. They aren't meant to be anyone's role model."

As Cici gave her final thoughts on her interview,

Cambria reached for the remote and shut the television off. Her blood roared with anger and righteous indignation. She felt the hot tears gathering in her eyes. Turning toward Greg, she asked, "Did you hear that?"

Glancing up from his book, he gave her a grim nod. "Pretty harsh, if you ask me."

"How dare Miles speak about me that way, after I agreed to use my vacation time to help further his cause?" She didn't say it aloud, but remembering the moments of passion they'd shared made his words cut even deeper. She wiped away a fallen tear and stood up.

"Let me guess. You want me to take you over there." Greg closed his book and set it on the small table beside him.

Locking eyes with her bodyguard, she nodded. "You read my mind." She jammed her feet into a pair of flat leather boots, grabbed her purse and followed Greg out the door.

As they drove southwest across town from Buckhead to Collier Heights, Cambria fought back the sob rising in her throat. She planned to go in there, metaphorical guns blazing, to give Miles the cursing out he deserved. Showing up with tears streaming down her face wouldn't do.

When they arrived, Greg parked at the curb in front of the building and opened her door. "Do you want me to come up there with you?"

Already headed inside, she shook her head. "I got it."

She strode right past the reception desk to the elevator bank, ignoring everyone she passed along the way. When she arrived on the fourth floor she went straight to his office. The door stood open, so she walked in. "Miles Woodson, you've got a lot of fucking nerve."

He looked up from his computer screen, his brow knotted with what appeared to be confusion. "Good morning to you, too. What's going on with you?"

She snorted a laugh. "I can't believe you're asking me that, since you apparently know me well enough to be speaking on me to reporters."

His gaze shifted up for a moment. "Did that interview air already? I haven't even seen it."

She stood over his desk, her arms folded over her chest. "Trust me, you didn't miss much. It's basically just you, talking about your charity work and talking trash about me."

He held up both his hands. "Hold on, now, I didn't…"

"Save it, Miles. If you didn't want smoke, you shouldn't have been lambasting me on national television."

"Lambasting? Who still uses that word?"

She narrowed her eyes. "You wanna talk semantics right now? Or you wanna explain why you were talking shit about me!"

He stood up then, a panicked expression on his face. "Can you keep your voice down, please?"

"Nope. I plan on being as loud as it takes for you to hear me right now." She slapped a hand on his desk. "I agree to do you a favor, and this is the thanks I get? I let you into my home, into my bed, and you would still dog me out for the whole world to hear?"

He pressed his hand against his temple. "I don't know how the network edited that interview because I haven't seen it. But from your reaction, I'm guessing they took me out of context, big-time."

She shook her head. "Don't try that with me, Miles. It was an audio interview. I heard you say that mess with your own mouth." Tears welled in her eyes again, and she cursed them, knowing her anger was quickly melting into sadness. "I just can't believe you would do this to me."

He walked around the desk, reaching out his hand. His voice was soft, his gaze affectionate as he spoke. "Cambria. Baby, let me explain…"

She jerked out of his reach. "No, Miles. You've lost any right you had to touch me. And don't call me baby."

He sighed, let his hand drop. "Can't we just talk about this like adults? Please?"

She brushed away the tears streaming down her face, and knowing he could see her crying renewed her anger. "There's nothing for us to talk about. But let me say this. Whatever we had going on, it's over." She turned and walked back to his office door, pausing in the doorway. "Don't worry. I'll still be there for the talent show. I made a promise to the kids, and they shouldn't have to suffer because their mentor is a jackass."

Without waiting for a response, she left. She could

hear him calling her name as the elevator doors closed; she ignored him.

It wasn't until she was safely tucked into the back seat of her SUV that she let the sobs overtake her.

Miles sat back down at his desk, resting his head in his hands. A few minutes ago, he'd been drafting an email to his personal shopper, to ask her availability to pick up the items for his sponsored families. Suddenly, Cambria had stormed in, making accusations.

What the hell just happened? I didn't even get to defend myself, not that I could have, since I haven't even seen the final version of the damn interview.

He was still sitting there, with his head pounding, when he heard someone enter his office. Glancing up, he was relieved to see his twin sister. "Hey, Teagan."

"Don't hey me, Miles." She walked over to his desk, staring directly at him. "You wanna tell me what the hell's going on right now?"

"What makes you think this isn't just a typical Thursday morning at the office?"

She pursed her lips. "Dude, you gotta be kidding me. I'll give you two reasons. First of all, I just saw Cambria leaving here, and she did not look happy. And second, you're tense. I'd appreciate it if you got it together so I didn't have to…"

"Feel my pain secondhand. I know, I know." He shook his head, releasing a bitter laugh. "Unfortunately it's gonna take more than an aspirin to break through this."

"Well, can you at least tell me what happened?" Teagan dropped into his guest chair, tossing one leg over the other. "Maybe I can help."

"I doubt it, but here goes." He relayed the heated, rather one-sided conversation he'd just had with Cambria. "I didn't even know what to say, because she caught me off guard, and because I still haven't seen the stupid interview."

Teagan took out her phone. "Let's pull it up and take a look. I'm sure it's online somewhere."

He came around the desk, standing next to her while she searched for the video.

"Here it is." She tapped the play icon.

They watched the five-minute clip in silence. When it ended, Teagan looked up at her brother. "Yikes. If you said those things about me on TV, I'd be pissed, too."

He raked his palm over his face. "That's just it. I didn't say those things, at least not in that context. They edited my words, probably to make the interview more controversial."

Teagan blew out a breath. "Damn, bro. Not sure how you're gonna fix this one, other than complaining to the network or the show's producers."

"Even doing that probably isn't going to help me as far as Cambria is concerned." He sighed. "I can't even deal with this right now, because there's way too much going on. How's Mama doing? I haven't seen or heard from her in like a week now."

Teagan leaned forward in her chair. "She seems to be swinging back and forth between anger and sadness, really." She shook her head. "She's basically quit her planning work for the anniversary gala, and passed it off to me and Nia."

He groaned. "This is really getting out of hand. We have to figure out some way to get Mom and Dad to talk. He's probably going to be getting out of the hospital soon."

"Yeah. I just wish my man was in town instead of touring with Lenny Kravitz."

"How much longer till Maxton gets home?"

She appeared to be counting mentally. "Let's see… The tour is six weeks, he's been gone four, so…he should be back in a couple of weeks, unless he decides to bail out early and let the alternate take his spot onstage." She blew out a breath. "I could sure use his special brand of stress relief right about now."

Miles cringed. "Nah. Don't gross me out right now." He went back to his chair and sat down. "What a day."

"Meanwhile, when were you going to tell me you were in love with her?"

Well, that came outta nowhere. His eyes widened. "What? I never said…"

"You didn't have to say it." She shook her head, rolling her eyes. "How many times do I gotta tell you that I feel your emotions, before you believe it?" She clapped her hands together. "When we were kids, and I had a crush on a boy, didn't you get a stomachache?"

He thought back on their younger days. "Yeah. I can remember that happening a few times."

"The same thing would happen to me whenever some girl had your nose wide open. Couldn't hardly eat once it got serious." She tapped her chin. "Fast forward to adulthood. Didn't you know when I was going through it with Maxton?"

"Yes, but…"

"And didn't you feel it when I fell in love with him?"

He frowned. "I…guess I did feel something. Just a subtle change…"

"But you noticed it, didn't you?"

"I did."

She tilted her head to the right, eyeing him pointedly. "I rest my case. You love her, and don't try to deny it because my twin sense is undefeated."

He reclined his chair as far back as it would go, and stared at the ceiling. "I will neither confirm nor deny the validity of your 'twin sense' on this particular subject." He rubbed his throbbing temple while he counted the dots in the ceiling tile above him. "Either way, it doesn't matter how I feel about Cambria. I know how she feels about me. She hates me."

"*Hate* seems a strong word. You've only been around each other for a couple of weeks."

He scoffed. "You didn't hear her in here, reading me for filth a while ago. I'm probably her least favorite person on earth right now."

Teagan was quiet for a few moments. When she spoke again, she asked sympathetically, "What are you gonna do now? The feelings you have for her aren't just gonna go away, you know."

"I know." He swallowed. "But I need to shift my focus. I need to do what I can to stem the tide of drama happening in and around this family right now. That means focusing on the talent show, trying to help Mom and Dad quietly resolve this Keegan Woodbine mess—" he paused, feeling the sadness squeeze his heart "—and forgetting about Cambria."

"Hmm." Teagan stood. "That all sounds super honorable…and super unrealistic." She chuckled dryly. "Still, though, I'm here. I'll try to help out in whatever way you need me to."

He shifted his gaze from the ceiling to his sister's face. "Thank you, Teagan."

She grinned. "You're welcome." Making a fist and tapping her chest with it, she added, "It's all love with me, no matter how annoying you are."

As she slipped from the room, Miles shook his head. *She never misses an opportunity to be a brat.* Still, he loved his sister and he was glad to have her in his corner, especially at a time like this.

He was on a lyrics site, one that provided transcripts of the words in a song, as well as interpretation of the meaning. He'd found the page for Cambria's song "Love Language," and reading the description, he realized he'd been pretty far off on the song's underlying message.

I always thought this song was about a romantic relationship. Turns out it's about her love for herself. Seeing the lyrics spelled out and broken down onscreen helped to break through his preconceived notions, especially since the site had appended a short video clip of Cambria explaining her intentions with the song.

"It was all about self-love. Taking the time to discover what made my heart smile, and then doing those things for myself." Cambria shifted on the barstool she sat on. "Who's got time to wait for Prince Charming? I deserve to be loved on in the present, even if that means I gotta do it myself."

After watching the video, he remained at his desk for what seemed like hours, staring out the window. His whole world seemed to be flipped on its head, and he had no idea how he would set things right again.

Sixteen

Cambria opened her eyes against the sunlight Friday morning, and sighed. After an entire night spent chasing sleep that never came, she didn't feel rested at all, just frustrated.

She turned over onto her back, staring at the ceiling above. Her head throbbed, and the tension gathered in her neck and shoulders made a dull pain radiate through her upper body.

Rolling out of bed, she headed to the bathroom. Under the stream of hot water in the shower, she let the tears flow once again, as they had during the night.

Slipping into a fluffy robe and slippers, she went to the kitchen for something to eat, but found she didn't have much appetite. Settling for a cup of hot tea and a granola bar, she settled back into bed with her morning snack.

By the time she'd finished, she found herself back to staring at the ceiling. Yesterday, when she'd marched into Miles's office with fire in her eyes, she'd been overcome by anger and offense. Now, as a new day began, that initial anger had dissolved into sadness and despair.

She blew out a breath. *I'm not gonna spend all day in this bed. I need to get out of here, clear my mind.* Reaching a decision, she grabbed her phone from the nightstand.

Aunt Lisa answered her call on the second ring. "Morning, Cambria. How are you?"

"Not so good," she admitted. "Things are just, really rough right now."

"I'm guessing you finally got a look at that interview, then."

"I did. And I confronted Miles about the things he said, too."

Her aunt's tone turned sympathetic. "I'm sorry, honey. When I told you to enjoy his company, I never expected it to go this way."

"Don't apologize, Aunt Lisa. It's not your fault."

"I know you're upset. I can hear it in your voice." Lisa lowered her voice a bit. "Do you want to talk about it?"

"I can't. Not yet." The pain was simply too raw now, and she didn't want to relive it by explaining things, not even to her trusted confidante. "I need to get away, spend some time alone. So I'm going home to Vegas for a few days. You know, to clear my head."

"When are you coming back?"

"Probably Sunday or Monday. I'll definitely be back in town before the talent show." She sniffled. "Listen, can you let Granny know?"

"Sure, I'll tell her. Go on, take some time and get yourself together."

"Thanks. I love you, Aunt Lisa."

"I love you, too, Cambria. Call me when you're ready to talk."

"I will," she promised before disconnecting the call.

Out of bed once again, she went into the closet to find some comfortable traveling clothes. Settling on a pair of white jeans, a green sweater and brown leather booties, she got dressed and wrestled her curls into a low bun.

She found Greg napping in his chair in the living room. Gently shaking him awake, she said, "Morning, Greg. Can you take me to the airport?"

"Morning." He sat up, making eye contact with her as he came awake. "Where are we going?"

"Home to Vegas."

He nodded, stifling a yawn. "Gimme a few minutes to get a bag together and let the pilot know."

Within the hour, they arrived at the private hangar Cambria rented at Hartsfield-Jackson International Airport. There, Greg parked her SUV in the designated slip inside the hangar, then escorted her to her small private plane.

They were in the air by midmorning, and arrived at another private hangar at the airport in Las Vegas in the early afternoon.

In the black sedan she kept for travel when she was home, she leaned back against the seat and took in the desert scenery along the route. The orange-and-gold landscape of Nevada was the opposite of the verdant green of the South. Grass was replaced by gravel and sand, and instead of magnolia and azaleas, cacti and boulders provided the ornamentation along the sides of the road. The familiar scenery of the famed Las Vegas Strip, lined with its many themed hotels and casinos, gave her the comforting sense of returning home. While she wasn't interested in gambling or in navigating through crowds of tourists, she did enjoy visiting some of the upscale, world-class spas in hotels in the area. *I'm not sure I feel like hitting up the spa this trip, though.*

Traveling north and west across the city, they headed for Cambria's main home in the swanky suburb of Centennial Hills. She'd purchased the land in a quiet subdivision five years prior, along with the plots to the left, right and rear, to maintain a degree of privacy and separation from her neighbors.

The two-level home, fashioned of stucco and stone in muted shades of gray and tan, had five bedrooms and three bathrooms. It was large, but not a mansion by any stretch, and she considered it a good investment considering the area's robust real estate market.

She smiled as Greg pushed the button in the headliner, opened the three-car garage and parked the sedan in the last empty spot inside. Getting out, she passed by her other two vehicles—a silver extended cab pickup truck and a Can-Am Outlander 450 all-terrain vehicle—on the way to the side door.

Inside her kitchen for the first time in months, she opened the fridge. It was fully stocked, indicating the regular visits made by her housekeeper. She reached inside and grabbed a bottle of water and an orange.

Greg, walking in behind her, asked, "What are we doing while we're here, boss lady?"

Peeling her orange, she shrugged. "I don't know just yet. For right now, you can chill. I'll let you know what I decide."

"Cool." He headed for the window seat in the kitchen. "I'm on to the second book in the series, so I'm good."

While he read, she snacked on the orange and enjoyed the feeling of being back home, even if it was under less-than-ideal circumstances. She thought about everything that had happened over the past couple of weeks, and it made her feel a mixture of emotions. She'd been surprised to hear from Blaine, yet there was no way she could have anticipated that taking his call that day would lead to all this.

It took me so long to take a vacation. And when I finally do, my time off turns out to be just as dramatic as the time I spent on the road. Go figure.

She stared out her kitchen window, past her gauzy curtains. The houses across the street soon gave way to rocky tundra, then to the jagged mountains rising in the distance. She drained the last of her water, then crushed her empty bottle, tossing it in the recycling bin. "I think I know what I want to do, Greg."

He closed his book and looked her way. "I'm listening."

"I wanna go out riding. I haven't fired up that ATV in ages."

He chuckled. "Let me guess. Seven Magic Mountains?"

She grinned, despite the lingering sadness she felt over Miles's betrayal. "Yep."

Greg dutifully loaded the ATV into the bed of her pickup while she went up to her bedroom and changed into jeans, a long-sleeved shirt, a leather jacket and motorcycle boots.

Ninety minutes later, she secured her helmet and climbed atop the seat of her ATV. Just a few hundred yards behind her, the colorful stacked boulders, a public art piece by Swiss artist Ugo Rondinone, towered thirty feet above the Ivanpah Valley. Ahead of her the dusty terrain dotted with cacti and woody shrubbery stretched toward the mountains beyond.

Starting the engine, she felt and heard it roar beneath her. And she knew that, at least for the next few hours, she could set her tears aside to lose herself in the sights and sounds of the Mojave.

"Please tell me y'all know where the instructions are."

"I'm sure we have it…somewhere." Miles looked up from his seat on the floor, to see his sister-in-law standing in the doorway. Her hand rested on her belly, and her expression was one of concern.

Eden's gaze shifted to her husband's face. "Blaine?"

Leaning against the window frame, he patted the tool belt he wore around his waist. "I've got everything under control, baby."

"That's not what I asked you. I asked if you read the instructions." Eden folded her arms over her chest.

Blaine walked slowly across the room, navigating past the rubble before circling his arm around his wife's waist. "Honey, I promise to come and get you when we're finished. When you see everything all put together, you'll wonder why you ever questioned me."

She sighed. "If you say so, Blaine. I'm counting on you to make sure the baby has a cozy, safe place to sleep."

He kissed her on the forehead as he gently nudged her from the room. Turning back to his brother, he whispered, "Have you seen the instructions?"

Miles shrugged. "They're under...all of this." He gestured around at the pile of wooden parts lying all over the floor. "But honestly, I haven't come across them yet."

"Sheesh." Blaine swiped his hand over his head as he reentered the room fully, stepping over and around the scattered parts.

Miles took a deep breath, staring down at the mess around him. They'd unboxed the set, which included parts for both a changing table and a crib, around an hour ago, and the process of sorting was still ongoing.

This wasn't how I intended to spend my morning. But I did need the distraction. Gage had volunteered to go to the hospital for their dad, so that left Miles free to help his brother with this little carpentry project.

He could still hear Cambria's angry words echoing in his mind, still feel the guilt that had consumed him when he realized what he'd done. A single, split-second decision to take a call from a reporter and answer her questions had led to this whole mess. Yes, she'd taken his words out of context. But he knew she couldn't have done that if he'd simply turned down her request to interview him in the first place.

"Yo." Blaine snapped his fingers. "Earth to Miles."

He shook his head, returning his focus to the moment at hand. "What did you say?"

"I said, I think you're sitting on the directions, man."

He looked down, and saw the white pages jutting from beneath his right hip. "At least we know where they are now." He laughed while rising onto his knees and grabbing the booklet.

Blaine took the booklet, scooting some things aside so he could sit next to his brother on the floor. He opened it and pointed to the diagrams on the first page. "All right. Let's get these pieces grouped together by item."

While they sorted the pieces into piles for the

crib and the changing table, across the room from each other, Miles asked, "Which one are we building first?"

"The changing table. It has fewer parts and will probably be faster."

They spent a few minutes reading over the instructions, then tackled the table, assembling it piece by piece. With each turn of the hex key, Miles pushed away thoughts of Cambria, of the look on her face, the tears standing in her beautiful brown eyes.

It took a little over an hour, but they finally triumphed, ending up with a fully assembled, polished cherry changing table.

"Go in the closet," Blaine said, gesturing toward the sliding door, "and grab that little changing pad thingy. It's on the shelf."

He went into the closet and looked up. Seeing the furry, mint-colored item, he pulled it down and took it to his brother, who placed it atop the table. "Done. Now, let's handle the crib."

While Blaine stuffed the cardboard and plastic wrap from the changing table into a large black garbage bag, Miles pulled out his phone and opened a dating app. As he scrolled through profile after profile, he told himself that this was for the best, that he should simply go back to casual dating with women he could easily impress.

Blaine appeared next to him, peering over his shoulder. "You're on uDates? That's extremely pitiful, my dude."

He shrugged. "Don't be so judgmental."

"I'm not. I'm just letting you know this is a bad idea." He moved past him and began locating the numbered pieces of the crib, while referring to the diagram in his hand. "You're hurt right now, and you surfing that app is obviously a poor attempt at hiding your pain."

Miles closed the app and pocketed his phone. "So, you say this is a cry for help. Why are you roasting me, then?"

"I'm not, Miles." His brother gave his shoulder a squeeze. "All I'm saying is, whatever you had going on with Cambria is still fresh in your mind. Stop trying to go around it. Work through it." He gestured to the crib pieces at his feet. "That's why I asked you to help me, and sent Gage to the hospital. I figured you'd need something else to focus on, something physical."

He frowned. "You mean it's not because Gage is clumsy?"

Blaine laughed. "Okay, that's part of it, too. The last time I tried to do a project with Gage, he ended up drilling a hole in the toe of one of my boots by mistake."

Miles chuckled in spite of his sour mood. "Damn. It's worse than I thought."

"Look. I know it's rough right now. But I just want you to focus on what we're doing, okay?"

He nodded. "Yeah, I'm with you. I'm sure I'll get at least a hundred 'cool uncle' points for putting this stuff together for the kid, right?"

"At least." Blaine grinned, handing him a screwdriver. "Now hold on to this. You can screw the base pieces together once I stand them up."

He nodded, letting his eyes sweep around the room. It was painted a soft shade of yellow, since his brother and sister-in-law wanted to wait until their child was born to learn the gender. Standing in this room, which would soon be fully transformed into the nursery for his first niece or nephew, reminded him of the importance of family and connectedness.

Meanwhile, his mother and father were at odds, and he didn't know if they could ever resolve their issues.

He didn't know where things would have gone with Cambria, had he not made his mistake. Right now, though, he did see a few bright spots among the dark and dramatic surroundings of his life. And one of them was this baby, whose birth he hoped might unite the Woodson family, once and for all.

So he put thoughts of Cambria out of his mind, focusing instead on helping make sure the baby had a comfortable place to sleep.

This I can help with. This much I can control.

Seventeen

Saturday afternoon, Cambria set up her laptop on the kitchen table inside her home, ensuring it was fully charged. She was expecting a video call from her attorney, and she needed the battery to last through the duration.

She was looking at boots on a designer's website when the video call came in. Switching windows, she answered it. "Hey, Dani."

Danielle Burton, Esq, her legal counsel for the last three years, offered a smile. "Hey, Cambria. How are you?" She wore a sunshine-yellow blazer with a black-and-white-striped shirt, which was all that was visible within the frame.

"Things have been a little hectic, but I'm okay."

Cambria took a sip from her water bottle. "What do you have for me?"

"A lot, actually." Dani took a deep breath and pushed the black, square rims of her glasses up her nose. "Upon my review of your financial records, I discovered that Harley has been funneling fifteen percent of your income into a separate account at Kingsbury Bank, one I'm assuming you had no knowledge of or access to."

She blinked. "I've never even heard of that bank, let alone having an account there."

"I thought as much." Dani shook her head. "This money was being skimmed off the top of all your receipts for the past two years."

Cambria pressed her hand to her temple. "I can't believe this."

"There's more, I'm afraid. The account at Kingsbury Bank has two account holders on it. One is Harley. The other is…Paul Harding."

Her stomach soured, and her mouth went dry. "You mean to tell me that my own father participated in embezzling money from me?"

Dani offered a grim nod. "I'm afraid so. I want you to know that I've already relieved Ms. Harrison of her duties, based on the permissions you gave me earlier to do so. I've informed the bank that no one other than you is to have access to your accounts until you've personally granted it. Reach out to them and they'll give you your new, unique access information."

"I'll take care of that today."

"I've also sent my aides to her office to collect any and all records we'll need to form our case, as I assume you'll want to press criminal charges."

"I absolutely do." She couldn't believe Harley would do something like this, but her father's betrayal cut even deeper than that of her former manager. "What about my father?"

"I didn't want to overstep the parameters you set for me, which really only pertained to Ms. Harrison." Dani paused. "I thought you might want to speak with him before deciding whether to press charges against him, so I'll leave that to you. This is a sensitive situation, so let me know how you'd like to proceed."

Cambria leaned back in her upholstered dining chair, and took a moment to process everything her lawyer had just shared. *So, just like that, I'm without a manager and I may have to take my elderly father to court.* "Thanks for your hard work, Dani. I'll reach out to my father and see if he has any kind of explanation for all this."

"Good luck with that, Cambria. And I'm sorry I couldn't give you better news, but at least now the problem can be resolved." She laced her fingers in front of her. "I'll wait to hear from you before proceeding with anything else."

"I appreciate that." After ending the video call, Cambria drained the rest of her water and released a deep sigh. Of all the things she'd expected to hear from her attorney, none of them had involved her father. This little development would force her to do something she hadn't done in months: call him.

She shut her laptop; her parents knew nothing of the technology involved in a video call, so she'd have to do this the old-fashioned way. Grabbing her cell, she opened her contacts, found her parents' landline number. Before dialing, she engaged her phone's "record call audio" feature.

He answered the phone on the first ring. "Harding residence."

"Dad, it's me."

He harrumphed. "Well, if it isn't the prodigal daughter herself. Must be snowing in hell if you're calling us."

"Haven't checked the forecast, so I wouldn't know." She took a deep breath, preparing to bring up the reason she'd phoned.

He spoke again before she had a chance to. "You know, you could call and check on us once in a while. We could be dead and you wouldn't even know it."

"You seem all right to me." She shook her head, recognizing his feeble attempt at a guilt trip. "Me not engaging with you is called a boundary. It protects you and Mom from all the ways I continually disappoint you, and it protects me from having to hear about it."

"There you go with all that therapist bullcrap. True healing is in the Lord, child."

She ignored that last statement. "Anyway, Dad, I'm calling to ask you why you were working with Harley to steal money from me."

He stammered for a moment. "You... I... That's a strong accusation."

"It's not an accusation, though. My attorney has all the proof necessary to show it for what it is—actual, factual theft."

The line grew silent for a long moment, causing her to wonder if the call had dropped.

"Yes, I did it," he finally admitted. "She'd put the money in the account, and take a little cut. The rest went to me and your mama. Ten percent of what you made. A tithe...just like the Bible says."

Trust Dad to bring the Bible into his foolishness. "So you admit you're a thief. I'm sure your Good Book has some kind of awful punishment for that."

"You're in no position to judge me, Jezebel."

"Whatever you say," she replied, her voice calm and even. She'd long since passed the point of caring what he thought of her, or of trying to earn the approval she knew he'd never give.

"And I'm not sorry, not in the least. We raised you, and you owe it to us, you little ingrate. All you gave us was trouble and strife. Never wanted to mind us, never wanted to be the good Christian girl we tried to raise you as. Your mama and I deserve every dime I took, and more!"

"Okay. I understand." She paused. "You know, my lawyer said I should speak to you and hear your side, before I decided whether to press charges."

His tone changed from anger to fear. "Charges? You can't do that, not to your own flesh and blood."

She let loose the bitter laugh she felt building inside. "That's just it. I can, and I will. And since I've been recording this conversation, you just gave me even more evidence against you. So I hope you enjoyed the money, Dad. Because you won't be getting any more. I'll see you in court." Without waiting for a response, she ended the call.

I held my boundaries like a boss. My therapist is gonna be proud of me, even if my parents aren't. She felt the smile tipping her lips.

Her thoughts turned to Miles, and how this whole thing had been resolved thanks to his financial savvy, and his advice that she involve her attorney.

Truth be told, he was the only person who wasn't family or paid staff who'd looked out for her. Not just with the report, but in other ways. He'd held back on lovemaking because he sensed she needed rest, and he'd been open enough to share his pain while going through a family crisis.

She sighed.

Damn it. I miss him.

Miles's gaze rested on the stage inside the Celestine T. Woodson Memorial Theater, watching as two of his youngsters performed a magic act. Today marked one of the kids' final opportunities to perfect their various acts before the big talent show. The event would take place in just a few days, and the building excitement now neared its peak.

He sat three rows back, where he felt he'd have an optimal view of the stage, and did his best to pay attention as each performer or group of performers

did their thing. Now, five acts into this onstage rehearsal, he could feel himself fading. The more time
passed, the harder it became to maintain his interest.

*What has she been doing these past couple of
days?*

He looked down at his phone, opening a social media app. Navigating to Cambria's page, he
scrolled through it, but she hadn't posted anything
since their last encounter. Sighing, he closed that app
and opened another.

Gage sat down in the seat next to him. Glancing
at his brother's phone, he shook his head. "You're
just as pitiful as Blaine said you were."

Quickly closing the app, he tucked the phone
away. "I thought you and Teagan were working on
the decorations?"

"We are. I'm just taking a break." His brother
chuckled. "I wanted to see some of the kids' talents.
I didn't expect to find you here, being an internet
creeper."

Miles rolled his eyes. "If you came here to tease
me, save your breath. There's nothing you can say
that's gonna make me more miserable than I already
am."

Gage reached over and patted his shoulder.
"Miles, I'm not gonna clown you too hard, bro. I
can see you're suffering."

"Mr. Woodson!"

Both men turned toward the shout, which had
originated from the stage in front of them.

Brandy, balancing her two batons on her hips,

said, "I meant Mr. Miles. How come you aren't pay-ing attention to me?"

He sighed. "My bad, Brandy. I got distracted."

"You've been distracted all day," added Jackson, poking his head from around the curtain in the back-stage area.

Feeling properly chastised, Miles cringed. "Sorry about that, y'all. Go ahead, Brandy. You have my full attention, I promise." True to his word, he concen-trated on the children and their performances, until the last one left the stage forty-six minutes later.

Gage whistled. "Wow. These kids have got some really impressive skills."

"I know." Miles could feel the pride swell his chest. "The hard part will be trimming the acts so the show stays within the planned two-hour time frame." He paused. "That has to account for all fif-teen contestants, plus time for the SWATZ Girls to perform three songs." Thinking about the group in-evitably turned his thoughts back to Cambria. Trying to shake those memories off, he stood and gestured to his brother. "Gage, come with me. Let's see what Teagan is up to."

"We'd better. She can't be left unsupervised for too long." With a laugh, Gage got up and followed him.

Stopping by the backstage area, Miles gathered the children and their parents. "Before you all head home, I just want to tell you I'm really impressed with our acts, and I can't wait to see the final results. Good job, everyone."

The two men left the theater and walked the corridor until they spotted Teagan. Perched on a step-ladder, she was pinning talent show related items to the bulletin board just beyond the lobby. Seeing them approach, she smiled. "Hey, y'all. How did the rehearsals go?"

"Great," Miles answered. "The kids really do have a lot of talent, and I know it's gonna be a great show."

"He's right." Gage reached out to catch a pushpin his sister dropped, and handed it back to her. "Once we help Miles get his shit together, it's bound to be a magical night."

He cut his eyes at his brother. "Damn, Gage."

Gage shrugged. "You're a mess. And since you're in charge of this whole enterprise, we need to fix that."

Teagan stepped down from the step stool, using it as a seat. "I agree." Looking up at him, she asked, "Miles, have you spoken to Cambria since she came by your office that day?"

He shook his head, anticipating the shellacking to come.

"Have you even tried reaching out to her?" Gage watched him expectantly. "Have you texted, called, sent up smoke signals?"

"No, I haven't. I think she made it pretty clear she doesn't want to talk to me."

"Did you at least find out anything about what she's up to while you were nosing around on her social media?"

He rolled his eyes. "No, Gage. I didn't."

"So basically you haven't really tried to fix things, then." Teagan sucked her teeth, an indication of her annoyance. "She was mad when she came to see you, but she has to have cooled off by now."

"Whatever. I don't have any way of knowing that, and I can't risk setting her off right now." He threw up his hands. "If I make her mad again, and she backs out of the talent show this late in the game, I'm royally screwed."

Silence fell among the three of them, and Miles listened to the sounds of the kids and their parents, their chatter and footsteps echoing in the building as they left for the evening. Hearing them made him think of those families he'd pledged to help for the holidays, and how they deserved to receive what they'd applied for. "If she doesn't show up, I'll have to refund all those tickets, and my holiday project will be dead in the water."

Gage piped up then. "Listen, I'll make a deal with you. If you reach out to Cambria and she backs out, I'll foot the bill."

Miles turned wide eyes to his brother. "Are you serious? You do understand the amount you'd have to make up is in the low five figures, right?"

Gage cringed, but nodded. "Yes. It's been a while since I made a big donation to the foundation, so let's just call it that. I mean, if it comes to that."

Teagan grinned. "That's a very generous offer. I'm proud of you, G."

"Don't be. I'll be praying extra hard that Cambria

accepts his apology, so I don't have to part with ten stacks." Gage laughed.

"Then we'd better help him come up with an approach." Teagan tapped her chin. "You know he's no good at this kind of thing."

Leaning against the wall, Miles looked between his older brother and his minutes-younger twin sister, and he could only smile. "I love y'all, I swear I do. And I know y'all love me back. But y'all have the most annoying way of showing it."

Teagan's grin only widened. "Whatever. The point is you obviously need us to bail your ass out of a sling."

"Yep. Again," Gage added.

Miles eased down to a sitting position on the polished floor between his brother and sister. "All right, you two. Tell me how to do this, then."

Eighteen

Cambria lay across her sofa, trying to find a comfortable position. On the console table across the room, she'd put on the vinyl of Pete Rock & CL Smooth's 1992 album *Mecca and the Soul Brother*. To her mind, the eight-track opus stood out as one of hip-hop's most foundational works. Pete's effortless flow, backed by CL's ad-libbing and the smooth, midtempo jazz-infused music filled the space.

Digital just doesn't come close to capturing this sound quality. Bobbing her head to the music, she grabbed her phone and made a call.

"Hey, honey." Her aunt's voice held a smile. "What's going on?"

"Remember how you said to call you when I was ready to talk? Well, I am, and I've got a lot to say."

"I'm listening."

"Let's start with the latest developments first." Cambria spent a few minutes explaining her lawyer's findings, including Paul's involvement.

Lisa sighed. "I knew my brother was terrible, but I had no idea it went this deep. It's bad enough he does nothing to help take care of Mama. But to take money from you, too?"

"He's a special kind of terrible." Cambria shook her head, remembering their conversation. "Luckily, I'm done trying to win his favor. Now it's his turn to try and win mine…or at least the judge's."

"Are you pressing criminal charges against him?"

"Nah. The old man won't last a day in jail. I'm going the civil route." She shifted her position so she could look out the window. A neighbor passed by, walking a Yorkie on a bright blue leash. "Who knows if I'll actually recoup any money. I just need him to face some consequences for his actions."

"Good. If there's one thing my brother hasn't had nearly enough of, it's consequences." Lisa cleared her throat. "So, what about all this drama with Miles? Tell me what's going on with that."

Cambria explained the way she'd dressed him down for slandering her during the interview. "I haven't heard from him since."

"That interview certainly painted you in a negative light. That's why I called you as soon as I saw it."

"You weren't the only one. My phone was lit up like Times Square that morning."

"I can understand why you'd be angry about the things he said, at least initially. How do you feel about it now?"

She sighed. "Hurt, mainly. It's not the first time someone has talked crap about me publicly and I'm sure it won't be the last. But this one really hurt." She couldn't articulate it out loud, but Miles's words had felt like a personal betrayal, whereas most of the others had seemed like mere opportunistic clout chasing at her expense.

"Hmm. This is a tough one."

"Yeah, it is. What makes it even tougher is, I miss him."

Aunt Lisa asked, "If he called, would you talk to him?"

"At this point, yes." She blew out a breath. "I just don't think I can be the one to reach out. The circumstances are just too complex."

"I can understand that. I don't know if I'd reach out to him, either, all things considered." Lisa's voice became muffled for a moment, then cleared up again. "Your grandmother wants to talk to you."

"Okay, put her on."

"Sugar Plum?"

She smiled. "Hey, Granny. How are you feeling?"

"I'm all right, but I miss you, lamb. When are you coming back to Atlanta?"

"I'll be back in time for Sunday dinner," she promised.

"All right, then. Bring me something nice from out there, you hear?"

She laughed. "Yes, Gran. I'll bring you a cool souvenir, I promise." Anticipating her request, she'd already planned to hit up one of the boutiques off the beaten path, to get another addition to her grandmother's shot glass collection.

"Okay, then. I love you. I'm gonna put your aunt back on."

"Love you, too, Granny."

Lisa's voice came over the line again. "I'll let you go, unless you have anything else to tell me."

"No, that was pretty much it. I'll grab you something while I'm out shopping for Granny."

"Thanks, Cambria. And just so you know, I won't be offended if you swing by the Coach outlet for my souvenir."

Shaking her head, she laughed. "Bye, Aunt Lisa."

After she disconnected the call, she sat up and set her phone down. Her aunt's advice had been clear, though not explicitly stated. Let Miles reach out, and give him a chance to explain himself. Considering how much she missed him, she knew she'd probably end up folding the moment he apologized.

But right now, she had no way of knowing if that apology would ever come.

When Miles stepped off the flight at the Las Vegas airport, he slid his phone from his pocket and disabled airplane mode. The signal began picking up as he walked down the concourse with his lone duffel, and he saw the half dozen texts from his siblings, asking if he'd arrived yet. Pulling them all into a group text, he responded.

Chill out, I'm here. I'll let you know how it goes.

Once he'd gotten his rental car, he headed into the city to make a quick stop. He completed his errand and then engaged the GPS, following the directions as he headed to the city's northwestern corner. As he drove, he did his best to calm his own frazzled nerves.

I'm following Teagan and Gage's elaborate ass advice. So, if this all blows up in my face, I blame them.

His only consolation was the knowledge that at least if things went to the left, he'd be able to turn his brother upside down and shake him for all the money he'd pledged.

Parking in the paved driveway, he walked up to the big two-story house, with a bouquet of pink roses in his hands. He gave the home a good once-over, marveling at its Southwestern architecture. The stonework and clean, modern lines made the structure appear striking and homey all at the same time. Walking beneath the tall, column-flanked archway to the front door, he rang the doorbell.

Greg opened the door, eyeing him. "Hello again, Mr. Woodson."

"Hey, Greg." He shifted his weight nervously from one foot to the other.

"You can't be surprised that I answered the door." Greg folded his arms over his chest.

He shook his head. "I'm not. When her aunt Lisa told me where she was, she also warned me that she wouldn't be alone, and that if I tried any foolishness, you'd expose my vital organs to daylight."

He nodded. "She's absolutely right."

"I didn't doubt her for a minute."

"Then I'm impressed you still showed up here." He glanced over his shoulder. "Wait here. I'll let her know you're here. *If* she wants to see you, she'll come to the door. But if she doesn't…"

He held up one hand. "I'll leave willingly. No need to stuff me into my car or anything."

Greg shut the door, and Miles could hear him walking away. The muffled sounds of their voices traveled through the door for a couple of minutes, before silence fell again.

The door swung open again, and to his relief, Cambria stood on the other side. "Hey, Miles."

"Hey." He found himself staring at her. She was dressed in a pair of ripped jeans and a black Ramones T-shirt knotted at the waist, the sleeves revealing her tattooed arms. *She's so gorgeous, no matter what she wears.* "These are for you." He extended the bouquet her way.

"Thank you." She accepted the flowers, bringing them to her nose for a sniff. "These are beautiful, I love them."

"I'm so glad you said that." He pointed at his rental, sitting in the driveway. "Because there are nine dozen more of them in the car."

Her eyes widened. "You're not serious."

He chuckled. "I'm afraid I'm very serious. Do you have someone to help me carry them in?"

Still wide-eyed, she said, "I guess Greg can help." She called her guard to the door. When he appeared at her side, she nodded toward the driveway. "Mr. Extra here says he's got nine dozen roses in the car for me."

Greg whistled. "Oh, he's apologizing big-time, then."

Miles unlocked the car, and he and the big man managed to get all the flowers into the house in one trip. While searching her kitchen cabinets for vases, Cambria said, "Who told you to do this?"

"What makes you think it wasn't my idea, to buy a single small florist out of every pink rose she had in stock?"

Cambria laughed. "This doesn't seem like your MO. You had help, admit it."

He sighed. "All right. My siblings gave me the idea, and your aunt told me your favorite color."

"Gotta love Aunt Lisa," Greg quipped as he added water to the growing group of crystal vases on the counter.

Miles stood in the dining room, watching them take care of the flowers, praying that Cambria's easy manner, along with the fact she'd let him in the house, were good signs that he had a chance at earning her forgiveness.

She walked over to the table, her bare feet hardly registering a sound on the soft carpet. She sat down and gestured for him to sit across from her. "I'm guessing you want to talk. I'm ready to listen."

"I do." He sat, taking his phone from his pocket. "The first thing I want to do is let you listen to something. It's the full audio of my interview with Cici Castellano." He queued up the sound file on his phone. "After everything that happened, I called the show's producers to complain. In exchange for not suing them for gross misrepresentation, I got them to send me the unedited version." He placed the phone in the center of the table, turned up the sound and let it play.

While they listened, he watched the expressions playing over her face. There were moments of recognition and of confusion, and by the end of the recording, realization.

When the recording ended, he grabbed his phone and tucked it away again. "Now you've heard everything that was said." He stopped, taking a deep breath. "I need to admit to you that I've been very judgmental about you and your music in the past. I took some time to sit down, listen to your songs again, read the lyrics and really take in the meaning. I was wrong to think of your art in such a reductive way, and I'm sorry for that. But you need to know the producers manipulated the interview recording, and this was the best way to prove that."

She blinked several times, her chest rising and falling in time with her breaths. "They really did edit it to make it sound like you didn't like me. Why would they do that? There are plenty of people who are vocal about their disapproval of me that they could have asked. They would be happy to bash me on national TV."

He shrugged. "I honestly don't know. Maybe it was just because the talent show has tied our names together of late." He paused. "I can't say I care about their motivation. All I care about is that you know the truth—I didn't bad-mouth you to that reporter."

Her hand flew to her mouth. "And I acted like that in your office that day... I'm so sorry, Miles."

He shook his head. "No, baby, I'm sorry." Getting up, he walked around to her side of the table and knelt by her chair. "I'm sorry I treated you the way I did. I was critical at every turn. I gave you every reason to believe I'd speak against your name." He took her hand in his, gave it a gentle squeeze. "And I'm sorry I didn't tell you that I've fallen in love with you."

She sniffled. "You've got to stop joking with me like that."

"I'm very serious." He stared into her eyes. "I love you, Cambria Harding. Every improper, irreverent, tattooed inch of you."

Tears filled her eyes as she leaned into him whispering, "I love you, too, damn it." She slid out of her chair and into his arms.

There on the soft carpet, he held her close to his heart, nuzzling his face into her curls and inhaling the sweet fragrance of her.

Nineteen

Cambria sat at the table facing the stage Friday night, enjoying the opening act for the 404 Cares Talent Show. The young teen telling jokes about school and the odd social strata his peers adhered to was funny, but still family-friendly.

He's doing a great job warming up the crowd.

Behind her, all three hundred seats inside the community center's theater room were filled, and she could hear the periodic laughter that accompanied each of the young man's expertly delivered punch lines.

Flanking her at the table were a city councilman and a local clothing store owner, who made up the rest of the judging panel. Somewhere in the crowd, Ainsley and Eden were also enjoying the show, but she couldn't turn around to look for them, lest the performers think they had less than her full attention.

She felt the boutique owner elbow her gently. "This young man is pretty funny!"

"That he is," she agreed before turning her attention back to the stage as the first act was announced.

By the time the third act took the stage, Cambria could already tell she had her work cut out for her. The young people in this neighborhood seemed to have a lot of talent, in various capacities. That meant it wouldn't be easy to choose a winner and two runners-up to receive the trophies and gift cards being offered up as prizes.

As the talent portion of the show drew to its end, a DJ played music while the judges deliberated. Cambria had a hard time choosing her favorites, but eventually was able to pick three acts she thought deserved recognition.

Miles appeared onstage as the DJ faded the music. Cambria couldn't ignore how handsome he looked in his dark suit, red vest and red paisley tie. "I want to thank all the talented young people who participated in tonight's show, as well as all of you who bought tickets to attend. You've helped to make it a happy holiday for a lot of families in need, right here in Atlanta."

Cheers erupted from the crowd.

He continued as the excitement died down. "Before we hear the winners of tonight's competition, I just want to share the total amount of money raised by this event. One hundred percent of this money will go directly to use for forty-one families." He paused, then quoted an amount in the five figures. Another round of boisterous applause met that announcement, and Cambria joined in, as well.

"Now, I'll pass it over to the judges, who will announce the winners." He walked to the edge of the stage and handed the cordless mic to Cambria.

She accepted it, then stood and turned to face the crowd. Another round of cheers went up, and a few people yelled out her name. "Thank you for that enthusiasm. I'm so happy I agreed to be here for this show, because I'm very impressed with the talent I've seen displayed here tonight. Right now, I'd like to announce the winners of the competition."

The room fell silent as she took the card handed to her by the councilman, and read the names and their corresponding placement out loud. The three youngsters reported to the stage, and the councilman joined them there to give them their trophies and the one-hundred-dollar gift cards that came along with them.

Miles retook the stage again and announced, "We'll now have a brief intermission while the SWATZ Girls get ready to rock the stage."

The house lights were brought up, and people in the theater began to get up and move around their seats. Excusing herself from the judges table, Cambria slipped out of the theater through the side door, then entered a small multipurpose room a few doors down the corridor.

Eden and Ainsley were inside the room, and when

Cambria walked in, she caught Ainsley helping her cousin into her dress for the performance.

"You need help? Or you got it?"

Ainsley shook her head. "I told her she would need some room for her belly to breathe." She unzipped the dress, waiting until Eden stepped out of it, then flung it over the back of a nearby chair. "Luckily I got her a secondary costume, so she can match us without feeling so restricted."

"Cool." She walked past them to the makeshift closet, which was just a long clothing rack on wheels, and grabbed her dress. It was a stunning cocktail-length dress in a dark shade of shimmering blue.

Soon they were all dressed. All their outfits were the same color, but the style of each varied. Cambria in her strapless cocktail dress, Eden in a pantsuit with a long bedazzled top and high-waisted pants with hidden tummy support, and Ainsley in a glittery, long-sleeved maxi dress with a high slit that showed off her leg.

Circling up, they held hands and Eden said a brief affirmation. "We came not to play, but to slay."

When they parted, they made their way to the stage. The curtain had been closed to allow them to position themselves. Ainsley and Cambria helped Eden onto her stool, then went to the mic stands flanking her.

Cambria took a deep breath as they were announced, and as the curtains slid open and the music began to play, she looked out on the crowd and raised the mic to her lips. "Y'all ready for this reunion?"

Shouts and applause filled the space as the girls went into their biggest hit, "Take Your Time With Me." She quickly fell into the groove, moving in tandem with Ainsley through the steps, all the while aware of Eden's seated position as they navigated around her.

They moved into "Sweet Like Candy," the song they'd been singing in the restaurant that day in the now viral video. Then they closed out their agreed-upon three-song set with their cover of Dionne Warwick's classic ballad "Walk On By."

As the house lights rose, Cambria saw that every audience member was on their feet. She brushed away the tears standing in her eyes.

Ainsley walked over and grabbed her by the waist. Shouting over the roar of the crowd, she said, "A standing O. Not too shabby for an old school group, huh?"

"Damn straight," Cambria replied. The two of them went to Eden's side, engaging in a group hug as the applause continued.

When Cambria stood again, her gaze sweeping over the theater, her eyes landed on Miles. He was cheering and clapping along with everyone else.

Their gazes met and locked.

She raised her hand to her mouth and blew him a kiss.

He pretended to catch it, pressing it to his own mouth with a wink.

She could only smile in response. She'd come here three weeks ago, exhausted, burnt out and ready to hide from the world. Yet he'd convinced her to perform, driven her to heal old wounds and, in the interim, allowed her to do some good for the city she loved.

He's an amazing man with an amazing heart.
And lucky me, he's all mine.

Miles sat by his father's bedside Saturday evening, as he'd done so many times over the last couple of weeks. With his phone in hand, he entertained himself by playing a puzzle game.

His dad had fallen asleep on an episode of *Law and Order SVU*, after having watched several in the network's weekend marathon of the popular crime show. Miles knew that if he so much as breathed on the remote, his dad would awaken and start yelling about how he'd simply been "resting his eyes," so he didn't bother with trying to change the channel, even though he was bored out of his mind.

He was conquering level twenty of the game, and contemplating spicing things up by sending Cambria a freaky text message, when the room door swung open. Looking up, he felt his jaw fall open. "Mom?"

"Hello, son." Addison walked in, with Nia close behind her. They closed the door, and as Nia joined Miles on the hard vinyl love seat, Addison went to her husband's bedside.

She reached for his hand and patted it softly. "Caleb, wake up."

He shifted a bit in bed, then opened his eyes.

"Addy?" He sat up, staring at her as if in disbelief. "Addy. You came." He reached for her.

She took a step back, but held on to his hand. "I'm not there yet, Caleb."

He dropped back against his pillows, but nodded his head. "Fair enough. I'm just glad you came to see me, darling."

Miles tugged the end of his sister's gray wool peacoat and whispered, "How did you get her to come here?"

Nia popped his hand and whispered a reply. "I didn't. She asked me to bring her here."

"Why?"

She popped him again. "Boy, hush and let them talk! Maybe if you do that you'll find out."

Not wanting any more of Nia's big sis energy, he closed his mouth and turned his attention back to his parents, who were speaking quietly to each other.

"I can't say that I'm okay with those test results. They cut me to my core." Addison placed her free hand over her heart. "And I also can't say I forgive you for lying to me. But I can say that I'm not ready to give up on this marriage, on this family."

Caleb's eyes filled with tears. "That's all I ask, Addy. That you give me a chance to make things right."

She nodded, but remained quiet.

"Listen. I know how this whole thing looks, but I swear to you. I never cheated on you, and Keegan is not my son."

Addison wiped away a tear of her own. "The test results say different, Caleb."

He nodded. "I know they do. What I don't know is why." He paused, sitting up straight in bed again. "If you talk to the doctor, he'll tell you how I ended up in this bed."

"What do you mean?"

"I know what he's talking about," Miles interjected. "I was here the other day when the cardiologist made his rounds. I asked him if he could identify a cause for Dad's heart attack, since it seemed to come out of nowhere."

"And what did he say, son?" His mother watched him intently.

"Shock. He said it was likely caused by shock." Miles clapped his hands together. "Meaning the test results surprised Dad just like they did the rest of us." Saying it out loud now, he realized he actually hadn't considered that his father was telling the truth, until that moment.

The room grew silent for a few moments, and Miles sensed everyone in the room turning his words over in their minds.

Addison nodded. "Maybe there is something amiss."

"There absolutely is, and I plan on getting to the bottom of it."

Caleb cleared his throat. "After they spring me from this joint, anyway."

Sitting down on the foot of the bed, Addison released a long exhale. "I think I can give you some time to iron this out, Caleb."

"Wonderful. When will you be coming back

home?" Caleb leaned forward, touching his wife's shoulder.

Her head dropped. "No, Caleb. I'm sorry, but I…I'm not ready to come home just yet. All I can offer you now is time to get this sorted out, and to prove to me that you didn't violate our vows."

Caleb slumped, but offered a solemn nod. "I understand. Where will you be in the meantime?"

"With Nia, for now. I may visit my sister up in Charlotte." She shrugged. "Do what you can to find out what's going on, Caleb."

"I will. I promise." He looked to his children. "There's only one thing I can think of, and it may sound a little far-fetched. Someone at the lab tampered with the results."

Nia tapped her chin. "I don't know. It doesn't sound that far-fetched to me. It would be a pretty clever way to extort someone."

Miles followed his sister's line of thinking, and suddenly, this whole mess began to make a lot more sense. "Nia's right. If Keegan, or somebody who put him up to this, thinks they can make a financial gain from this, why wouldn't they go to these lengths?"

For the first time in several days, Caleb smiled. "This is a gratifying moment for me. I've spent so many hours feeling like I'd gone insane, like no one believed me." He wiped his eyes. "You've probably all had your moments of thinking the worst of me. But this is what I've been waiting for."

Addison stood. "Nia, I'm ready to go."

"Okay, Mom." Nia crossed the room again, taking

her keys out of her coat pocket. As the two Woodson women headed for the door, Addison paused.

Turning around, she returned to the bedside and placed a soft, fleeting kiss on her husband's forehead. "I truly hope you can restore my faith in you, Caleb."

Nia and Miles exchanged a quick grin.

On the heels of her words, she and her daughter departed.

Miles looked into his father's smiling face. "All right, Dad. You've gotta get better so we can put this paternity mess to rest, once and for all."

Caleb nodded, his expression conveying his determination. "You're absolutely right, son."

Twenty

Navigating through the thick crowd of revelers, Cambria made her way to the table hosting the punch bowl. She grabbed one of the paper cups, ladled up some of the bright green concoction and poured it into the cup.

Miles eased up behind her, winding his arms around her waist. "So, how are you enjoying our annual Spooky Spectacular, Mary Jane?"

She turned in his arms and placed a quick peck on his red-fabric-covered cheek. Shouting to be heard over the pounding music, she answered, "It's great, Spiderman."

She glanced around at the multipurpose room illuminated by the orange specialty lighting. Paper cutouts of pumpkins, skeletons and other ghoulish images festooned the walls, beneath the orange-and-black streamer that hung from the ceiling.

He fixed himself a cup of punch and they headed for the east wall of the room, where a row of folding chairs had been placed for those who wanted a break from the dance floor. It took some doing to get through the tangle of bodies and flailing limbs, but they finally made it.

Miles sat in the only available seat, and she dropped easily into his lap. Pulling up his mask and sipping from his cup of punch, he frowned. "This kiwi stuff tastes a little weird to me."

"It just tastes fruity to me." She sniffed it. "It's not spiked, is it?"

He shook his head. "Nah. We just usually have watermelon punch, so the difference is really noticeable."

She looked out over the dance floor, at the hundred or so costumed people shaking their tail feathers to Ray Parker Jr.'s classic *Ghostbusters* theme. Her formerly short vacation was now stretching into its second month, and she couldn't remember the last time she'd felt so rested and refreshed. "I'm so glad I extended my time off."

"You needed it, after all that nonstop touring." He finished the punch, crushed the cup and tossed it into a nearby trash bin. "I've really enjoyed spending all this time with you."

"It's been amazing." She flung her arm around his shoulder and gave him a squeeze. "I just wish the photogs would give it a rest. They've been hot on my tail for the last couple of weeks, but that happens every time I stay in one place too long."

He chuckled. "Yeah. Perils of being famous, I guess."

"And now that you're always up under me, you're gonna keep getting photographed, too." She tweaked his nose.

"It's a small price to pay to be with the woman of my dreams."

She grinned. "I see you're laying it on thick tonight."

He winked. "I'm just getting started, baby. Got a lot more tricks up my sleeve."

A shiver went down her spine as she recalled just how talented he was. Leaning in, she whispered, "You already have my panties in your pocket. What more could you have planned?"

"You'll see," he whispered back, his face revealing nothing. "Just be patient."

They sat together for a while, watching the party go on around them. When she heard one of her favorite hip-hop songs from the early aughts come over the speakers, she jumped up. "Come on, Peter. Let's dance!"

He put up little protest as she tugged him out onto the dance floor. They were out there through four fast songs before the DJ threw on Ready for the World's "Love You Down."

As they swayed to the music, she enjoyed the feel of being wrapped in his arms. A bright flash of light sparked in her periphery, and she turned her head to the right. A man in a frog costume stood among the crowd, aiming an expensive camera in their direction.

"Well, shit." Miles shook his head. "Looks like one got in."

She frowned. "I can't believe one of these creeps made it past my security team." She released her grip on Miles and turned toward the frog photographer.

Before she could open her mouth to curse him out, Miles grabbed her hand. She turned her attention back to him. "What is it?"

The music stopped, and the people around them began to back away, leaving them a wide berth.

"I may have let him in," Miles admitted, a guilty look on his face.

She pursed her lips. "Why would you do that?"

"So he could capture this moment." Taking a step back, he knelt before her and slid a small box out of a hidden pocket in his costume. Opening the box, he said, "Cambria Harding, will you be my wife?"

Her hands flew to her mouth, and a sob escaped instead of an answer. Tears flooded her eyes, blurring her vision.

Still kneeling, Miles laughed. "I hope those are happy tears."

She nodded, finally reclaiming her voice. "They are, you goofball." She gave him a playful punch in the shoulder.

"So, is that a yes?" He raised the box, letting her get a good view of the princess-cut pink diamond solitaire.

She nodded again. "Yes, Miles. Yes."

He slipped the ring onto her finger, and cheers erupted around them as he took her into his strong arms and kissed her.

The camera flashed again, probably joined by fifty or so phone cameras, but she didn't care.

She was about to marry the man of her dreams.

One week later

Miles stood in the white stone Terrazza Di Sogno on the property of Las Vegas's Bellagio Resort, trying to hold back his tears. Across the terrace, Cambria walked toward him, escorted by her grandmother. She wore a floor-length, mermaid-style strapless gown that hugged every curve of her body and displayed her tattoos the way an expensive frame displayed a piece of fine artwork. Holding a bouquet of pink roses, she moved slowly in his direction.

Time seemed to stand still as he waited for her to arrive. They'd timed the wedding to take place in the evening, and the sun was now a fiery orange ball, touching the horizon in the distance. All around them, the Strip was coming alive with the sights and sounds of Vegas nightlife. But none of the things happening around them held a candle to the sight of his radiant bride.

"You all right, bro?" Gage, his best man, teased from his left. "Your knees knockin'."

"Get it together," Blaine, his other best man, chided from his right.

Why did I choose to let both of these clowns stand up here with me today? Miles shook his head, straightening the collar of his dove gray tuxedo. He decided not to dignify his brothers' teasing with a verbal response. After all, Cambria was meant to be the center of attention now, and as she came into his personal space, he forgot anyone else was even present.

Soon, their hands were joined as the officiants said the words. Twenty guests looked on as they exchanged solemn promises of forever. They held up their rings before placing them on each other's fingers, to read the words inscribed inside aloud.

"You are my melody," he said as he slipped her ring on.

"You are my harmony." She slid the ring onto his finger, twisting it a bit to get the diamond-encrusted band past his knuckle.

The ceremony continued, ending when they were announced as husband and wife. Tugging her body close to his, he raised her chin and planted a kiss on her lips that sealed their vows and laid bare his love for her.

The party then moved across the terrace, to an area where tables and chairs had been set up, along with their wedding cake and light refreshments. The air, cool and crisp as evening faded into night, was heavy with the smell of rich food and champagne.

Sitting at the main table with his new bride, he

placed his arm around her shoulders. "I'm so glad I didn't have to share you today."

She nodded. "Me, too. Granting an exclusive pre-wedding shoot to *ONE Magazine* was a stroke of genius."

"I'll take credit for that idea," he said, giving a mock bow.

She rolled her eyes. "You're a mess. It cost us a mint, but it was totally worth the extra security to keep prying eyes outta here today."

"Right." He glanced out at their families, mingling and eating before them. "It's nice to see everybody together, especially after all the drama my family has been dealing with."

"It's been wild for both of us lately. At least I'm gonna get some restitution from my dad. I mean, eventually."

"It'll help defray the cost of the security, right?"

"I guess that's one way to look at it." She giggled. "It's all up from here, honey. I feel it in my heart."

He pulled her close to him. "That's all the reassurance I need."

"I love you, Miles."

"I love you too, Songbird." He placed his lips against hers, and let himself be overcome by the peace only she could give him.

* * * * *

*Thanks to violinist Megan Han's one-night fling with her
father's new CFO, Daniel Pak, she's pregnant! No one
can know the truth—especially not her matchmaking
dad, who'd demand marriage. If only her commitment-
phobic not-so-ex lover would open his heart…*

Read on for a sneak peek at
One Night Only
by Jayci Lee.

The sway of Megan's hips mesmerized him as she glided
down the walkway ahead of him. He caught up with her
in three long strides and placed his hand on her lower
back. His nostrils flared as he caught a whiff of her sweet
floral scent, and reason slipped out of his mind.

He had been determined to keep his distance since
the night she came over to his place. He didn't want to
betray Mr. Han's trust further. And it wouldn't be easy
for Megan to keep another secret from her father. The
last thing he wanted was to add to her already full plate.
But when he saw her standing in the garden tonight—a
vision in her flowing red dress—he knew he would crawl
through burning coal to have her again.

She reached for his hand, and he threaded his fingers through hers, and she pulled them into a shadowy alcove and pressed her back against the wall. He placed his hands on either side of her head and stared at her face until his eyes adjusted to the dark. He sucked in a sharp breath when she slid her palms over his chest and wrapped her arms around his neck.

"I don't want to burden you with another secret to keep from your father." He held himself in check even as desire pumped through his veins.

"I think fighting this attraction between us is the bigger burden," she whispered. His head dipped toward her of its own volition, and she wet her lips. "What are you doing, Daniel?"

"Surviving," he said, his voice a low growl. "Because I can't live through another night without having you."

She smiled then—a sensual, triumphant smile—and he was lost.

Don't miss what happens next in…
One Night Only
by Jayci Lee.

Available December 2022 wherever
Harlequin Desire books and ebooks are sold.

Harlequin.com